To HELEN,

R.J. Barrett

12-25-2021

Mystery of the Windowed Closet

by

R. J. Bonett

Cover design drawn by: Ronald J. Bonett

Grateful appreciation to: Marie Bonett, Mary Morris,
Bonnie Bell Hilfiger for content approval.

Kandace Rollman Wortz: Editor.

Karen Delise: Assistant for front cover.
New York Camera & Video Photo restoration
1139 Street Road
Southampton, Pa. 18966

Disclaimer: This is a work of fiction. All characters and events
are purely fictional. Businesses, locations and organizations
while real, are used in a way that is purely fictional.

Forward

Ray Bishop, a 35 year old high end insurance underwriter for Keystone, buys an abandoned 100 acre farm in Bradford County Pennsylvania.

Arriving on a stormy night the first weekend in October, he was confronted by a horse and wagon coming in his direction. As the wagon passed he noticed the driver appeared to be staring angrily at him. The woman with him was looking straight ahead seemingly in a catatonic state. Why was he angry? Perhaps the man had wanted to buy this farm?

The dash across the muddy road to the shelter of the front porch would only add to the mystery. When he turns to look, a flash of lightning reveals the carriage was gone. Could it have gone that far in such a short time?

Entering the house gave him an eerie feeling of foreboding. He knew old houses were drafty, but the feeling of cool breezes across his face seemed to follow him from room to room. Then there's the closet on the second floor at the top of the stairs that defies logic. Who would build a closet with a window?

Being awaken from a deep sleep by a clap of thunder, a flash of lightning reveals an image of a woman gliding across the living room. As she passes the front window, another flash of lightening reveals she's transparent. Startled by the event, he gets out of his sleeping bag and watches as she climbs the stairs entering the closet with the window. Hesitatingly; he climbs the stairs too. Slowly opening the door, there's nothing in the room.

But wait: Did he hear the moaning wail of a crying child? Only with the help of a psychic friend and a series of séances, will the house reveal the deep dark secrets it harbors.

Chapter 1

It was beginning to get dark early for mid-October that damp rainy Thursday afternoon. I was standing at the window of my fourth floor office at the insurance company, looking out over the city. It had been raining all day with a heavy cloud cover in place that hung over the city like a shroud. The rain was an all day miserable rain, a rain that would normally on your day off, give you second thoughts about getting out of a warm bed.

I was anxiously awaiting a phone call from a client about his commercial liability policy. The only sound in the room breaking the silence was the clicking of the pen against my chin as I leaned against the wall in deep thought. I was concentrating on what problems my client might encounter, problems that might give my boss second thoughts about me writing the policy.

Had I missed anything? Had I connected all the dots in the event of a civil action? Maybe there was a problem I haven't thought of? Will he be underinsured? He's building a five- story building in center city. He's built other structures before without difficulty so there shouldn't be a problem.

Whenever I worked on a policy of this magnitude, a little voice would come forward from the back of my mind and constantly torment me with the same questions. It was there every time. It was my own voice disembodied and repeating. Are you sure? Are you sure? Silencing that voice always required an overpowering force pushing it to the back of my mind, and it was always a challenge.

At 35, with almost 11 years in the company, I didn't need to prove anything. I had considered every imaginable scenario he might encounter, and yes, I was satisfied.

"Yes damn it! I'm sure!"

Had I said that aloud? I looked toward the door, expecting a knock or a buzz from our receptionist on the extension, asking if there was any problem. Suddenly, my mind changed gears, and I found myself looking down on the business signs across the street. With the fog and misty rain, the signs had a hazy appearance, and only being familiar with the different stores could I identify what they were. I had done a lot of thinking, planning and even second-guessing looking out that window.

I watched as the rain began to come down harder and its impact on the street below. People were moving faster, scurrying up and down the sidewalk, trying to protect themselves from the rain. Most were hidden under umbrellas that were unfurled and moving in a frenetic pace. The sea of canopies was occasionally broken by the few without umbrellas, wading out into the sea- holding newspapers over their heads as their only protection. Looking down on them, they resembled a mass state of confusion, weaving in and out of each other in no organized manner. I also took note that the street traffic was quickly building up, even at this early hour.

Just then the phone rang. "Hello, Ray Bishop, Keystone Insurance. How can I help you?"

It was Ted Arnold, my reason for staying late that rainy afternoon. All he needed was my reassurance that his risk was covered, and I was suddenly relieved that I had done my homework; and as the insurance slogan goes, he was in good hands. There was some small talk about the lousy weather, carefully avoiding the business rhetoric, and then the pause. Time to get to the point!

"Yes Ted, thanks for getting back to me. I've gone over your current coverage thoroughly, and I'm sorry to say," hesitating intentionally for effect, then laughed to put him at ease. "That as much as I tried to raise your premium on this renewal, it looks like your coverage should be sufficient for another year."

Now it was his turn to laugh, and I sensed his relief.

"So you're good to go, and good luck on that project." I said, knowing I could have pumped up the price of his coverage as he apparently expected, padding my own commission. "Thanks for your business."

Hanging up the phone as he signed off, I hurriedly tried to organize the paperwork strewn on my desk, returning them to their relevant folders. Periodically, my boss, Mr. Johnson, would wander in the room, and I didn't want him to see anything out of place or policies not put back into file cabinets.

Mr. Johnson has been my overseer since I advanced to writing higher- end policies about eight years ago. I believe he was grooming me for his position when he retires in the not -to- distant future. The responsibility is considerably more, but the pay increase was well worth it and the reason I could afford the farm.

He's been a fixture in the company for over 40 years and keeps it running like the fine movement of a Swiss clock. His wife passed away three years ago, and he seemed to try making up the hollow feeling by burying himself in his work. He was always the first to arrive each morning and the last to leave every night. Always making sure the coffee pot was on every morning, and the aroma was always much welcomed. Yes, he was the last of the old guard when wearing a suit with a white shirt and bowtie were fashionable.

But today, my schedule was clear, and I was hoping I wouldn't get another client's phone call- or an assignment from him before I could leave.

If I could only get out of the office a little sooner, I could beat the traffic onto the Pennsylvania Turnpike. Grabbing my jacket and umbrella, I made a quick survey of the room before turning out the light and closing the door behind me. The fourth floor is where most of the larger business transactions took place, and the hall outside the elevator was crowded.

"Hi, Ray, why the rush?" It was Les Walton, a friend from underwriting who was also waiting for the elevator.

"I'm off tomorrow, Les. I want to get ahead of traffic," I said, looking around nervously like a shoplifter trying to get away from the scene of a crime. "I'm going to the farm."

The conversations of the people waiting for the elevator dissipated as I uttered those words, and several people turned to look at me with interest.

"What's this with a farm? Are you leaving us?" He looked familiar I'd seen him in the building, but he didn't work on the fourth floor.

"No, I'm not leaving. I bought a farm in Bradford County during the summer." I said, lowering my voice. "I'm heading up there now."

"What's this with a farm?" asked another person I knew.

"I bought a farm in Bradford County during the summer for my retirement. It's northwest of Scranton, beautiful country; and the view from my front porch is spectacular." Repeating my words, "I'm heading up there now."

Walton jerked his head back over his right shoulder. "You better take the stairs. I saw your boss, Mr. Johnson, looking for you."

"Thanks for the warning," I said with a wink.

I ducked down, looking between the heads of the people waiting, and saw Mr. Johnson standing on his toes in the doorway of my office, stretching his short frame, examining the group waiting for the elevator to see if I was among them.

He just missed catching me leaving the office by only a few minutes. Turning up my collar, and bending slightly at the knees trying not to be noticed, I pushed open the fire escape door, and hurriedly went down the four flights of stairs to the lobby of the building.

A man I knew, Warren Simmons from property and casualty- who can only be classified as the ultimate office nerd, was walking through the lobby. Slight of frame and always wearing clothes that somehow seemed to be too big, his appearance was complimented by wearing thick glasses.

Warren always seemed to go from office to office, deeply engrossed in reading a contract, and more than once collided with a water fountain or missed a doorway by several feet. Everyone that knew Warren always gave him a wide berth.

People would often chide him about his poor navigational skills and say, "Warren, if you drove like you walk through this building, there isn't an insurance company in the country that would insure you." He always looked at them as though he was trying to figure out whether it was something he should really be concerned with. He was walking toward the bank of elevators when he suddenly looked up. "Hey, Ray, Mr. Johnson's looking for you."

"Do you know why, Warren? It isn't something I forgot, is it?" I asked, my heart sinking but making an effort to appear nonchalant. "Do you know whether it was something urgent?"

"I don't think so. I think it's about a customer he wants you to handle."

"Look, if he sees me, it'll tie me up for at least an hour. I'm off tomorrow, and I'm trying to get an early start for a long weekend. Do me a favor. Don't tell him you saw me, Ok? I'll owe you one."

"That's a deal. Going to that farm?"

I realized I probably told a dozen people max, but word sure got around fast. It was the same way when I got a divorce. It seemed like keeping a secret in the company was a monumental task, if you didn't want it out, you couldn't trust telling anyone.

"Yeah, it's the first weekend I'll be able to stay at the house."

"Be careful driving," he said, looking over his shoulder walking toward the bank of elevators. "The weather looks pretty crappy."

"You bet. Thanks again for the warning."

The 240- mile drive that late in the afternoon wasn't something I was looking forward to, especially with the rain. Yet, I was excited about getting away and being able to spend the weekend there offset the misery of the long journey.

Dealing with some customers in the insurance business isn't physical, but sometimes mentally demanding, especially when they hear a price for a certain type of policy. You're actually selling something they may never use- that neither one of you want to have to use- and at a considerable price.

I was responsible for writing the high end policies of the company. Most of the people I dealt with were wheeler dealers who knew how to negotiate and get the most from their investments. A great deal of responsibility goes with it, but the financial end is more rewarding and the reason I was able to purchase the farm.

With a light rain, traffic getting to the turnpike would be slower than normal, but with the rain coming down at this rate, it would only make things worse. I thought, "If I could only beat the rush hour traffic." I waited in the doorway for the traffic on the street to stop, then popped open my umbrella and darted between the cars to the parking garage across the street.

Shaking the water off my umbrella then closing it, I threw it in the back seat. I already had my sleeping bag and overnight bag in the car and was ready to go.

After the first two exits from the city where most of the population lived, the traffic would be a little lighter, and I could be a little more relaxed, listening to classical music on the radio. I pulled out onto the street and successfully navigated my way through it to the turnpike.

Finally getting past the rush hour traffic, I settled comfortably back in my seat, tuning the radio to a station that catered to the light classical listeners.

About a hundred miles from the city, the radio signal began to fade and was slowly being replaced by static. I thought… 'I wish someone, someday, will invent a radio signal that goes farther than a hundred miles.' I switched the radio off, silencing the static. To break the monotony of the windshield wipers clearing the rain, I entertained myself by thinking about the farm and the initial reason why I bought it.

Even though I dealt with high rollers on occasion, I had never been big on financial planning. I just decided that it's never too early to begin investing in something besides a retirement account- especially an investment for the future when I retire in about 30 years. I knew I didn't want to live in the city after retirement, but how would I handle a complete reversal of 180 degrees from what I had become accustomed to?

I knew it was a gamble, and just like any other gamble, there's no such thing as a sure bet. After all, the business I'm in; the insurance business; is actually a gamble: a risk that a customer won't need the policy he's paying for.

For the present, the farm's a hobby I know I'll enjoy, and with the condition it's in, the hobby would probably take a few years to complete.

To say it was a fixer upper would be an exaggeration, a severe understatement. It would put my natural talents as a handyman to the test, as well as taxing my energy and patience. And yet, it could prove rehabilitative too, and the source of a great deal of satisfaction. I definitely needed my life rehabilitated, and I hadn't been satisfied in anything I'd done in a long time.

I don't know for sure, but I guess that's the reason Jennifer, my ex, divorced me. She wanted a house at the New Jersey shore, but when I bought the farm, she became irritable. When I began to get gardening books in the mail and books on how to raise chickens and beef cows, I guess that was the last straw, *Straw*. I laughed to myself. Now that's funny. *Straw*, another association with a farm, something she absolutely hated.

At the end of our marriage, I used to really get under her skin humming the theme song from an old television series, Green Acres. The plot was a sophisticated woman who marries a common guy who buys a farm- wanting to return to his roots. Exactly our situation, with one exception, she sticks it out through thick and thin.

I began laughing out loud, alone in the car. As I laughed, I began to sing: "You are my wife. Goodbye, city life. Green Acres we are there…" As I thought of the times I used to sing it to irritate her, I began to hum the theme song as I laughed. "Da… Da… Da… Dunt Dunt. Dant, Dant."

As hard as I tried, I could never quite picture her dressed in bib coveralls with a straw hat, gathering eggs in a hen house or working in a garden.

She was beautiful enough to be a model for a sensual picture on a calendar, with her long blond hair and shapely figure. She could have been a great advertising poster, like Betty Grable with her bent- over pose that lifted the spirits of so many men during the war, adorning many aircraft, ships, submarines and tanks.

Come to think about it, maybe I wasn't totally fair about the purchase of the property. But, oh well, I don't think either one of us would have fit in the others world of tomorrow. There's no sense hashing it out any longer- as they say, that's water under the bridge. Even if she would have given it a try for my sake, she still would need to have her nails painted and high heels. She could never in her life go completely "country."

I didn't understand why she didn't have any confidence in my ability to restore the place. I wasn't like some men who couldn't repair things and I proved it many times on different projects in the house she now owns. *Yes*, she now owns. She never had to call a plumber, carpenter or an electrician for anything she needed done.

Luckily, I learned everything I knew about tools and how to use them from my father. He was a patient, talented man who taught me so much. I had the natural talent too, thanks to his genes, and I could have been a hell of a contractor. He was wrong about one thing as I look back on it now. He was convinced I should go to college, and from there it was a business degree and then the job with Keystone. The security and money is great, but I don't really enjoy my work. My real satisfaction came from taking most of that money I earned and putting it into my house- I mean *her* house. But, despite the regrets, I'm glad she's gone.

I even hope she's enjoying the house I put so much work into. That's why I couldn't wait to finally get that all settled physically and emotionally. I was getting excited about finally resurrecting this place that been sitting there waiting for me.

There was something strange about that house. On one hand it was structurally sound, and I could see all kinds of remodeling possibilities. All the land that came with it was like having a country estate! And yet, there was something about the place- a strange foreboding. Was it something telling me to buy this particular place? Why this one? I had looked at so many properties. Was it pure luck that I stumbled on this property at such an amazing price? Why? The land alone was worth what I paid for the entire property, including the house, the barn and that strange little room at the top of the stairs.

Chapter 2

What's that ahead? Break lights? That's a flashing light from a police car. Traffic seems to be slowing down. Damn, I hope it's not an accident. I don't want to be tied up too long; it's getting late. We're almost to a stop here, with only two more exits before I get off. Ah, good, the traffic's beginning to move again. Whatever it was must be clear now.

Slowly moving forward with my blinking lights on, I could see a tractor- trailer off to the side of the road. It must have slid on the wet surface trying to negotiate the curve, and the trailer end was lying on its side with some of its contents spilled. Doesn't look like anyone's hurt. Thank God.

I thought of my ex, always complaining about the long ride and how it would be dangerous in the winter. Was it a legitimate concern for me? I couldn't tell. Of course, coming up here in the winter was something I wouldn't do, but I'm sure it was only another excuse not to like the place, of that I was certain. Especially after seeing the place in the condition it's in, and not being able to grasp its possibilities.

The traffic flow is picking up, and that should get me back on schedule. It would only be another 20 minutes before getting to the exit. Being familiar with the toll amount, I turned on the inside light and went through my pocket to get the exact change, putting it in the ashtray along with the ticket. Finally reaching the exit, I slowed down to negotiate the sharp turn on the rain- slick road and pulled up to the toll booth.

"Good Evening! I just drove up from Philadelphia. Has it been raining here all day?" I asked, making conversation with the toll collector as

I handed him the ticket and money. He made no attempt to conceal his boredom seemingly ignoring my question.

"Has it been raining here all day?" I repeated before he finally responded, "Let me see now. Not just today, but the last *three* days." A flutter of something approximating a smile came across his face. "Typical fall weather, how was the road coming up?"

"It's been raining in the city all day, but the trip up wasn't too bad. I did see a tractor- trailer lying on its side."

Suddenly looking up concerned, making eye contact for the first time he asked, "Where was that?"

"A couple of exits back. It looked like it just slid off the road. The police were there, and I didn't see any ambulances, so I guess nobody was hurt."

"That must be the one I heard about. The state police were through here a while ago and told us about it. They try and keep us informed about any changes, so we can alert drivers about traffic conditions. Here's your receipt. Thanks for letting me know. Have a nice weekend."

"Do you know anything about the road conditions going to Canton?"

He replied, "I'm not familiar with Canton. Where is it?"

"It's just past Towanda."

"I haven't heard anything, but be careful of the deer on the road. They're usually moving around quite a bit, it's their rut season."

"Yeah, I noticed a few that must have been hit lying on the side of the road on the way up. Have a nice night."

I was a little more than 50 miles from my final destination, as I pulled out on the secondary road for the last leg of my journey. Being dark with the rain coming down a little harder, dense patches of fog were in some of the small valleys on the winding road. Being in the mountains, the air was a little cooler, so I turned up the heater to compensate.

I put aside the thought of the conversation with the toll collector and refocused my mind on what the house would look like after I finished the reconstruction. It was built in the 1880s on an older foundation, that hadn't been mapped on any prior property descriptions. I surmised that, by a stone in the basement wall that read, "Smythe 1772". The stone is part of the stone steps that lead to the outside from the basement. The room was probably part of the foundation of a root cellar years ago, before the current house was built and probably used for storing vegetables after the harvest. It made more sense to enlarge the existing foundation and use it as part of the basement for the current house.

I secured the property through a realtor who represented the owner. He was from New Jersey and only purchased it two years before I bought it. I only met him once at the settlement and wondered why he was selling it again so soon.

He seemed to be a cold sort of fish, and when I asked about the property, he seemed reluctant to talk about the house or his reason for selling it, and I wondered why. I thought to myself, 'Maybe he was married to a Jennifer too.'

The house was a typical older style farmhouse. It was originally three rooms on the first floor and three bedrooms on the second, with a room I couldn't quite figure out. It couldn't have been a bedroom. It was too small. It looked more like a large closet. But why did it have a window? That's what puzzled me. I couldn't think of many good reasons, but I could think of many weird ones. I assumed someone living in the area, perhaps a descendant of one of the earlier occupants, would have a logical explanation.

The first floor had a living room, dining room and kitchen, and an extension on one side that was built years later. It probably served as an extra bedroom until they converted it to a bathroom after indoor plumbing was introduced. The kitchen had original handcrafted cabinets painted white. They extended to the ceiling and made the kitchen look rustic, giving it a unique personality. I wanted to salvage them for restoration, if it was at all possible.

I laughed again, as I thought of my ex, trying to function in that kitchen.

A coal furnace was in the middle of the dirt floor in the basement, and at some point years ago, it was converted to an oil burner as a source of heat. It worked, thanks to the previous owner's efforts on that front and

I knew during the reconstruction, it would be a major change, but for the time being, it would have to remain as I worked on other priorities.

At some point in the past, wooden shelves were built on one wall, resembling a corner pantry. They were used for storing Mason jars of food that was canned during the growing season. There were still a few on the shelves, but the lids and rims were rusted, and I couldn't identify the contents, but wasn't about to tempt fate and try sampling what was in them.

The barn across the road looked much older than the house, with its hand hewn beams and wooden pegs holding the joints together. Some of the beams were 20 feet in length, and with the adz marks visible, you could tell they were made when someone was straddling a log, slowly cutting away chunks to form the square beam. It told the tale of someone working hard to make a home and livelihood for himself and his family. Having a little knowledge about working with power tools, I knew what kind of effort was expended by the person that built the barn. Sorry to say, but through years of neglect and the roof leaking, some of the beams, along with the underlying structure in spots, were soft and rotted, and I knew the expense of restoring it would be prohibitive.

I remember the conversation standing in the barn with the realtor the day he was showing me the property for the first time. The sidewalls are missing a few boards, and the ones still there are split and weathered from age and have a grayish color to them.

Pigeons and barn swallows didn't have a problem entering without coming in through the open sliding door. They were nested everywhere. When we entered the barn, several pigeons took flight, but barn swallows being an aggressive bird, dive bombed us immediately, coming at our heads forcing us to duck.

After a few minutes, they realized we weren't a threat and seemed to settle down but always kept a watchful eye at how close we were to their nest.

The wind was whipping down the mountain that warm sunny day, coming through the open spaces where boards were missing. The realtor jokingly remarked, 'It's even air-conditioned.'

With a smile and a nod, I acknowledged him saying, "This barn's in pitiful condition. It's going to have to go."

"Do you know any contractors in the city? They might take the barn down for nothing, just for the old beams and boards. Some people like that rustic look."

"I use to know two, but they went out of business. It's hard to make a buck in that town."

"Why's that?"

Pulling on a rope suspended from a track in the ridge of the barn that was used to move hay bales, I replied, "Taxes are through the roof, and according to one of them, everyone has their hand in your pocket."

Giving me a strange look he asked, "What do you mean, 'Hand in your pocket?'"

"Every building inspector: the city with its taxes. He just couldn't take it anymore and wound up getting a job as a maintenance man at the airport. He doesn't have to worry about getting construction jobs, or any of the other crap he was forced to deal with. As a plus, he gets all the benefits of paid vacation, holidays, and free medical. It's a shame though. He was a good contractor."

The realtor seemed surprised and gave me a look of skepticism at what I was relating, but I assured him it was no exaggeration.

I remember him saying prodding me for a sale.

"Well, what do you think about the property?"

When I asked him about the generous price the owner was asking, he said something about the owner wanting a quick sale, and I just happened to come along at the right time.

"I think in spite of its faults, I'm always up for a challenge, especially one I can afford. I'll buy it. Let me get my checkbook from the car and write you a deposit." I remember it as though it happened yesterday. That was in early August.

Putting the conversation aside with the realtor the day I committed myself to buying, I found myself getting sleepy. With nothing to listen to, trying to stay awake was becoming a problem. I put my hand out the window to get it wet then rubbed it on my face. The cool air rushing in for the few seconds I had the window down, felt refreshing, temporarily rejuvenating me. I told myself, "Stay awake! Stay the hell awake. You'll be there soon."

The storm had intensified with flashes of lightning only seconds ahead of claps of thunder, but I was finally there, turning onto the road that led to the house. When I pulled up in front of the old barn, several sets of eyes greeted me. Being tired from working and the long drive, I was startled at first, but as they passed in front of the head lights, I could see they were deer crossing the road going into the nearby woods. I had seen no other deer out, thanks to the storm, so it spooked me a bit.

'What's the matter with you?' I thought, 'Afraid of your own shadow, afraid of a few deer that didn't have enough sense to stay in the thickness of the woods out of the storm?'

Reaching into the back seat, I got my sleeping bag and another bag with clothing I brought for the weekend. Anticipating getting out of the car, I waited for the next flash of lightning to see where the puddles were on the muddy road. I wanted to avoid stepping in them when I attempted to run for the shelter of the front porch, some 25 yards away.

With my hand on the door handle, I was about to fling it open when I saw something. It was a small red light that appeared on the road, coming in my direction. I turned the headlights on again to see what it was, blurred by the rain on the windshield. It's a horse and buggy. I was startled at first, but remembered the realtor telling me the Amish were moving into the area, and relaxed, assuming this was one of them. In fact, I was looking forward to meeting them and gaining some understanding of their lifestyle and apparent disdain for the things most other people find so important. I assumed they would be good people to have around when you had construction projects too big for one set of hands.

With another bright flash of lightning as the wagon passed, I could see what looked like a man dressed in black with a woman whom I could only distinguish by the white rim of her head piece. They seemed almost like an apparition, and as they went by, the man seemed to stare angrily at me, as though I was an intruder. The woman staring straight ahead looked catatonic and without expression.

The look of hatred chilled me to the core, and I thought to myself, 'I must be imagining what I'm seeing. I don't know anyone who lives here.' Thinking they were religious, I couldn't imagine why he would have any reason to stare at me like that. Thinking my mind was still playing tricks, I dismissed it. The rain was coming down harder now, and I laughed at myself again for acting like a frightened kid.

Grabbing my sleeping bag and clothing bag, I quickly flung open the car door, shouting, "Damn! Damn! Damn!" as I sprinted across the road, trying to miss the mud puddles. After reaching the porch, I turned to look. The wagon wasn't there; it was gone. Could it have gotten that far away in such a short time? I didn't know.

"Let me find this damn key." I dropped my bags and continued looking for it on my key ring. I thought to myself, 'Why have your office keys, your apartment key and car keys on the same ring? Why not get a separate key ring tomorrow and end the confusion of searching?' Between flashes of lightning, I was able to find the right key for the door, and after turning the knob, I went in.

The electricity was off due to the power outage, and the house wasn't only cold, but damp from all the rain. As the toll collector mentioned, 'It's been raining for three days.' ...and the cold dampness in the house verified his statement.

I was fortunate enough to think about bringing a flashlight and felt through my bag, finding it at the bottom. Lighting it didn't seem to add much illumination to the room. I thought, 'It would have been smart of you to try it before leaving home. You could have stopped on the way for batteries.'

Suddenly, I remembered finding a kerosene lantern in the basement on one of my prior visits. It was one thing left by a previous owner that actually worked. It should be on the kitchen table where I left it.

Going down the hall of the dark, damp chilly house, I was getting more help from the lightning flashes through the window than my flashlight. Walking into the kitchen, I spotted it right where I left it. So now I'm thinking, 'Hey genius, what are you going to light it with?'

I scanned the room with the dimming flashlight thinking, 'I'm in the kitchen, a country kitchen. They must have used matches to light things with. The stove had to be lit with a match.' I looked in all the cabinets and began to search the drawer's. There they are, in the stick match holder, hanging on the basement door next to the stove. Where else would they be, dummy?

With only the dull flashlight and surrounded by darkness, I thought I saw a shadow pass behind me and felt a cool breeze pass my face. Quickly turning, I scanned the room with my flashlight. No; nothing there. Suddenly a chill came over me and I shivered. I thought again, 'What's wrong with you, still afraid of the dark? I better get out of these wet clothes and put on my dry sweat suit.'

I struck the first match against the side of the match box. Damn, it didn't light, it broke in two. Let me try another. Two, three, four, I hope they aren't damp from being in this old house so long. Let me try again. Ah, finally, success! Now, how do I do this? I remember; you lift the globe, turn up the wick, and light it. With the slight smell of burning Kerosene as I put the match to the wick, the light became brighter, traveling to the remotest parts of the room, and I immediately felt more comfortable being able to see my surroundings. Scanning the room once more to make sure I was alone, I carried the lamp into the living room placing it on the small end table. The only other furniture in the room was a sofa I moved in several weeks ago.

It was close to midnight, and all I could think of was getting dried off, putting on dry sweat clothes, and getting into my sleeping bag. I already had it unrolled on the couch and adjusted for my comfort. Another chill suddenly went through my body with the wet clothes I still had on, and I immediately began searching my bag for dry clothes. Before I took off my wet pants and shirt I went to the front window to make sure no one was outside, then laughed at myself. The nearest neighbor is about a quarter mile away, and who would be out in this weather wanting to look in my window?

Slipping my wet clothes off, I wondered. 'Should I go back to the kitchen and hang these clothes over a chair to dry? Heck with it. I'll hang them on the door knob until morning.'

Pulling my dry sweat pants up and putting on my sweat shirt, I looked through my bag for my toothbrush and toothpaste. With the aid of the lantern, I was able to guide my way into the bathroom and get ready for bed. I turned on the water to brush, and in a few moments, the water slowed to a trickle. Damn! I forgot. The water pump is electric, it's off too. I should have brought a gallon of water. Luckily, I was able to finish brushing and returned to the living room. I extinguished the lantern and crawled into my awaiting sleeping bag, zipping it up like a caterpillar weaving a cocoon.

The only difference, in the morning I'll still be me and the house will still look like it does- a mess.

I repeated to myself the toll collector's remark. 'It's been raining for three days.' I don't know whether the electric was off all that time, but with the dampness in the house it sure feels like it. I reached over and turned down the lamp wick extinguishing the flame, then suddenly realized. What if no more matches light? I couldn't worry about that now. That will have to be on my priority list to buy tomorrow. Laying there with only my face outside my sleeping bag, I began to feel the warmth of my own body heat returning to normal.

I stared at the ceiling wondering about the Amish carriage that passed, and the driver angrily staring at me. Did I buy a property he wanted that maybe he couldn't afford? Maybe: But it's something I wasn't about to change, and that's for sure. How did the wagon disappear so fast? Again, I questioned whether I was imagining it. The whole episode began to seem very strange to me, and the thought that Amish people were always friendly began to come into question in my mind. I shifted my thinking, making a mental note of a few things I urgently needed from town in the morning. With the diminishing flashes of lightning temporarily illuminating the room and a very long day behind me, in a few minutes I drifted off to sleep.

Chapter 3

The next morning I was awakened by a knock on the front door. Looking at my watch; it was already 8 a.m. It felt like I had slept for 10 hours. I scrambled out of my sleeping bag to answer it. I opened the door to a man who identified himself as a neighbor. He was dressed in dungarees and had a blue quilted shirt covering his thin frame. His hands looked like the hands of a working man, cracked and in need of some sort of hand lotion. He was wearing a green baseball cap with the words John Deere printed across the front.

"My name's Frank," he said casually, getting right to the point. "I've seen that car here a few times before and wondered if you're the new owner?"

"Yes, I am! My name's Ray, Ray Bishop." as I extended my hand to shake his.

"Are you a farmer?" he asked.

"No, I live in Philadelphia and will only be coming up on weekends to work on the house."

He nodded with a reassuring approval. "If I can be of any help, just let me know," he said, giving my hand another firm grasp.

"Since you're a resident, can you tell me anything about the farm, or the people who lived here?"

"It was my mother and father's farm. Me, my brothers and sister were raised here."

"The guy I bought it from only owned it for two years," I said, stepping out on the porch letting the door close behind me. "Are there any major problems with the well water or anything else you might be able to tell me about? Something that maybe would cause me to have buyer's remorse?"

"No, the water is probably some of the best around. It doesn't have a sulfur smell or any other mineral problems that some hereabouts have. That fella that bought the house was going to use it for huntin. After buying it, I think he saw all the work that had to be done. I just figured he gave up on the idea." Crossing his arms, he smiled. "I think his wife might have been part of that decision. She sure didn't look like the kind that would even spend a night here."

I smiled back. "I know the feeling Frank. I think my wife took a hike for the same reason. I'm glad he sold though. It's just what I've been looking for the last few years. I like the view and the 60 acres of woods and the 40 acres of fields with the stream."

Smiling about my remark about my wife, he continued. "We always enjoyed living here as kids. Good luck with the property."

As he turned to walk away, I asked, "You mentioned other mineral problems with the water. What did you mean by that?"

"Some people hereabouts have methane in the water."

"How would you get rid of that?"

"The rule of thumb around here is, if the water looks clear, try it. If it tastes good and doesn't have a smell, it passes the test. Leave it alone. I don't think it's going to be a problem. Anyway, we never had a problem. I don't think you'll have one either."

"I hate to detain you with all the questions, but I heard the Amish were beginning to settle in the area. Have you ever had any problems with them?"

"No, no problems. They've been movin' in for the last several years, but unless there in need of something, they keep pretty much to themselves. Nice folks, though."

I told him about the ghostly carriage that passed last night when I arrived and the driver giving me an angry look. He looked puzzled at what I told him, and I could tell it took a few seconds for him to comprehend what I said. He looked like he was going to give me a response, but didn't say anything. As he turned again to leave, I asked, "Frank, one more question. Is there a restaurant close by?"

"There's one in Canton about four miles from here. It's called the Chatterbox. The food's pretty good."

"Care to join me? It's my treat."

"No thanks! I'm a little busy today."

He walked toward his vehicle, a red pickup truck skirted with fresh mud, and gave me a little wave without turning around.

With the look of bewilderment on Frank's face when I told him about the angry look from the carriage driver, I was happy I didn't elaborate and tell him the carriage seemed to disappear. Maybe he'd tell the rest of the neighbors I was some sort of kook.

After he walked off the front porch, I suddenly turned. The door was closed, and I wondered if I remembered to unlock it before stepping out. I thought, 'I may be calling Frank back for his help sooner than I expected.' Luckily, I remembered unlocking it and went back in.

After closing the door, I got my tooth brush to freshen up. The electricity was on and the water would be running again. I could hear the old furnace laboring, making noise, trying to crank out a little heat, and it felt like the house was beginning to dry out from the dampness. Happy the electricity was on again, I grabbed my tooth brush and went into the bathroom. Turning on the faucet, I cupped my hand, filling it with the cold running water. I sniffed it for any trace of sulfur and tasted it for purity. Frank was right. It passed the test.

After brushing, I put on my jacket and went outside. Although the air was cool, the sun shining on the wet leaves being in fall splendor, made the colors more vibrant. I walked down the hill where I parked the car outside the barn, enjoying the view of the valley flush with fall colors.

As I was getting in the car, I noticed the tire tracks from Frank's truck on the muddy road surface. Mine from the night before were only slightly visible, but there weren't any wagon tracks at all. No hoof prints either. I thought, 'That's strange. Being a narrower wheel, they should have made a deeper impression and still been visible.' Oh well, maybe something else passed over them.

I drove the four miles to town, passing well-manicured farms with stone walls meticulously stacked by creative hands.

They were erected years ago, when farmers were clearing fields for planting and used as markers, defining property boundaries. It all fit together like a picture perfect landscape painting. Once in a while, I would get a whiff of hickory smoke from farms where people were curing their own meat. Like the final touches on a work of art, it actually made the painting come to life- a life I was enjoying, even though it was only for a very short weekend.

The ride to town was quick, and I guess it was because I was enjoying the morning so much. I had a liberated feeling. Normally, I'd be busy in the office on Friday, and like everyone else working there, anticipating the weekend.

I must have been enjoying the scene immensely. Before I knew it, I was in town. There's only one major intersection with a traffic signal in Canton, and just beyond I could see the Chatterbox Restaurant sign, just as Frank described.

Canton's a small town with a population of about 2,000 people. It has a movie house from the turn of the century that appeared to be beautifully restored and appropriately called the Rialto, a traditional Italian name given to quite a few theatres at that time. I supposed it probably hosted vaudeville shows in its early years, then later silent movies, then talkies.

The Sentinel Newspaper, that's published weekly, stands across the street from the Canton National Bank. Like the Rialto, the bank's a granite stone monolith. A sturdy reminder from the past, where depositing your money was secure.

The little town boasted all the essentials, including a pharmacy, public library, high school and elementary school, grocery store and one of the favorites of outdoor loving locals, Jim's Sporting Goods.

Franklin Five and Ten Cent Store is at the intersection- a chain store that's been rapidly disappearing from the city. It also has a lumber yard, hardware store, and an establishment I knew I'd be visiting if I decided to go all in with raising my own chickens and beef cows. Rockwell's Mill, is at the North end of town. The large white building prominently displays its logo. Rockwell's, Feed, Grain, Hay and Farm Supplies. The few times I passed, there always seemed to be several pickup trucks being loaded with sacks of grain, or other farm commodities.

I parked in the small lot across the street from the Chatterbox and entered the restaurant. Scanning the crowded cigarette smoke filled room for an empty table, I spied one in a corner but hesitated, making sure I didn't have to be seated by a hostess. Surprisingly, my entry was acknowledged with a nod from people I didn't know, and I returned their gesture in kind. Still standing there, a waitress serving one of the tables looked up.

"Find yourself a seat. I'll be with you in a minute."

I weaved my way through a maze of tables to it, then slipped off my jacket and sat down. Taking a pen and paper from my pocket, I began to write a list of things I needed from the hardware store. I reminded myself to get matches, another flashlight, batteries, and a new key ring. Clicking the pen I thought, 'There were several other things I needed. Now what were they? I remember- padlocks, new door knobs and something else. Now what was it? I knew there's something else I urgently needed. That's it, light bulbs.'

I noticed a group of middle aged men in coveralls, and some were wearing red checkered hunting jackets, sitting at a large table in the center of the room.

They were having coffee talking to one another and must have been a regular group. They kidded with the waitress when she served their table, and she didn't seem intimidated by their remarks, answering them in a joking manner by name.

I sat amazed at people coming in or out, acknowledging each other with a hello and a few words of conversation, or a goodbye. I thought about the atmosphere of the place and the name of the restaurant was appropriate- *Chatterbox*! I looked down at the paper I was writing on and subconsciously wrote in block letters- CHATTERBOX, underlining it.

I was a doodler, a person who would fill in the letters on papers I didn't need that were on my desk at the office. Sometimes, I would block letter the person's name I was talking to on the phone. *Yes!* I was a true doodler. I thought about the Chatterbox being a real change from living in the city, a true micro culture of what I wanted after retiring, a cross section of people without the confusion of being better or having a nicer home than the next guy.

It seemed that I lived in the city all those years and never really got to know anyone other than my friends from work. I never knew my neighbors or even the woman whom I so passionately loved at one time who eventually became a stranger. This was something different. A typical small town I imagined, like many others across the country and unlike the city where you scarcely knew your neighbor. I was going to be happy being a part of it.

The waitress finally got to my table with two pots of coffee. "What will it be this morning, regular or decaf?" she said motioning with each in the appropriate order.

She was in her early 30s I guessed, with dark brown hair. Turning her head slightly she looked over my shoulder to read what I was writing.

"Looks like you have a regular shopping list there."

"Yes," I said, unaccustomed to such familiarity from someone I didn't know. "I have a few stops to make this morning."

"Sorry, I didn't mean to be nosey," she said without a trace of embarrassment. "It was hard not to notice."

"I'll have regular." She promptly poured it into a large mug. Not recognizing me, she took my order and noticed my accent.

"Are you from Philadelphia or New York?"

Smiling, I was amused at her being inquisitive. "I'm from Philadelphia. I'm not used to all this friendliness from people. It makes me suspicious."

Jokingly she replied, "You mean those fellas over there?" pointing in the direction of a crowded table of older men she obviously knew. "Don't mind them. They're a regular coffee clutch. They're all a little touched, but harmless."

They somehow heard what she said over all the other conversations in the room and the noise from the kitchen. One of them replied, "Don't believe anything she says. Ruthie lies a lot."

Quickly replying humorously, "I'll remember that next time you ask for coffee. I'll only pour half a cup- the other half just might wind up in your lap."

Half the restaurant laughed at the exchange of words, and someone at another table jokingly replied, "Ed: you might just as well forget it. You can't get ahead of her."

I laughed that the ice had been broken and began telling her about the farm.

"I didn't think you were the same fella. He came in here once or twice. My husband and me- we looked at that place a few years back, but it needed too much work. My husband can only hit his finger when it comes to a hammer, and we just didn't have the funds to fix it up right then."

I replied, "My ex-wife knows I'm good with tools, and didn't give me or the place a chance either."

She replied with what sounded like a theatrical voice. "Well, maybe that's why she's an ex."

I smiled. "Maybe you're right, getting back to your question. No, I'm the new owner. He sold it to me."

She replied, "I guess he took on too much work."

"Maybe- I'm curious about that. I spoke to a neighbor this morning. That was his opinion too."

"Which neighbor?"

"His name's Frank. Do you know him?"

"Sure do! Frank and his wife June__ nice folks, real nice."

"So June's his wife's name? I haven't met her yet. Thanks for telling me her name."

After breakfast, I paid the bill, and as I was getting ready to leave, the waitress who served me was serving another table close by. In the same theatrical voice she said, "Good luck with the farm. Nice meetin ya. Hope you come back real soon."

I gave her a nod of approval, and as I passed the table with the regular coffee group, one of the men seated stood up and put his hand forward to shake mine and I responded in kind with my hand.

"I heard you telling Ruthie you bought Wilber's old farm. I'm Ed, Ed Jones. Your neighbor Frank's a friend of mine. He told me someone else bought it. I guess it was you? I just wanted to say hello."

I introduced myself.

"Will you be moving in the place?" he asked. "It sure needs a hell of a lot of work. Sure does have a pretty view though."

"No, I'll only be coming up on weekends fixing the place, and you're right. It has a great view."

"Good luck with it."

I thought for a moment I might have heard him say as he was sitting back down, "You're going to need it!" but maybe it was my imagination.

Everyone at the table seemed to be attentive to our conversation, and it was almost quiet for the first time. As I was leaving, everyone at the table acknowledged me in some way.

As I walked down the street to the hardware store, I thought about the words I thought he uttered, 'You're going to need it!' Did I really hear that? Or was it imagined? I couldn't dwell on it. I had more important things to think about.

My first stop was the hardware store to get new locks for the front door, back door and a pad lock and chain for the outside basement door. I got some flash lights and batteries in case the power went out again, and for the same reason, a new wick for the lantern I used the night before. I also reminded myself to get another box of stick matches to light it with. I hadn't tried all the lights in the house, so I bought a pack of light bulbs just in case.

Checking out the items with the store owner, I learned he was a former New Jersey resident who moved to the area some 20 years ago.

"You'll be seeing me often," I said as he counted out my change. "There's so much to be done around the place."

He replied, "I can get almost anything you'll need. Thanks for your business."

Chapter 4

I returned to the farm and began replacing the door locks. Recent events- real or imagined- had made security one of my priorities. After I finished installing them, I spent the rest of the day pulling up the old carpets and piling them in the dining room. It was a dirtier job than I expected. I began ripping up the linoleum in the front bedroom when money started flying around the room. Where was this coming from? I looked, and there were still more $20 bills spread out on the wooden floor under the linoleum.

Examining a few of them, I noticed they were silver certificates in numerical order, dated 1932. Someone had put them there years ago and obviously forgot about them. I carefully pulled up the rest of the linoleum and counted the bills. $140- $160- No wait, there's a few more sticking out from under a loose floor board, two more, $200 hundred dollars all together. Maybe there's more under this loose board? I looked in and put my arm under as far as I could reach, feeling around at just an empty space.

My enthusiasm built, and like a treasure hunt, I began lifting up any loose board I could find in every room upstairs. As I searched hoping to find more treasure, my expectations were quickly dashed when I only found dust, and in one room, a few buttons that must have fallen through the floor boards years ago. Oh well, $200 is better than nothing, and being silver certificates, they'll probably bring another $200 or more from a collector.

I knew it wasn't unusual during the depression for people to hide money in their homes. At that time, no one trusted banks. I still had the downstairs to explore, so only briefly being let down, the downstairs may yet hold some secrets.

I never really noticed before, but there was definitely a lack of closet space. Maybe that's what the closet with a window was for, storage. After examining the bedrooms and small closets upstairs, I was still wondering about the closet with the window. I still couldn't figure it out, a room 5 x 7. I opened the door to it, and although the window was closed, there seemed to be a drafty chill that went across my face. With the sun shining through the window and the room being so small, it should have been warmer, and it didn't make sense. I closed the door again and went down stairs to continue my treasure hunt.

In the living room on my hands and knees, as I was trying to pull up a small piece of loose floor board, a shadow of someone standing behind me appeared. To my shock, the shadow on the floor looked like a man holding a hatchet. Startled, I quickly jumped up and turned around, but no one was there. Could it have been a shadow of a cloud passing by the sun that caused it? It looked awfully real. Dismissing it, I returned to my search which didn't yield any further treasure.

Getting a closer look at the rest of the downstairs rooms, I looked at the bathroom. It was an addition to the house and was in horrible condition. I dreaded having to take a shower in the tub without first scrubbing it clean. The kitchen has one door leading to an enclosed porch and a door on the opposite side of the room that led to the basement.

I could hear the furnace go on and off and wanted to go down to examine it, as well as the electrical box and the rest of the basement. I needed to know how much fuel was still in the oil tank to avoid running out when I close the house for the winter.

Opening the basement door, I suddenly jumped back, startled by a rat that was hiding behind an old broom on the landing. He stared up at me as though I was an intruder, and I quickly reacted by kicking it off the top step, not wanting it upstairs. "You're not allowed upstairs!" I shouted into the darkness of the cellar.

I was beginning to see why the previous owner sold after two years and briefly wondered if I took on to much also. I turned on the light switch for the basement, but no luck, the lights weren't working. I flipped the switch on and off a few times without success. Wait. I remembered I bought a pack of bulbs today. I'll see if that's the problem. Using my flashlight to guide my way down the stairs, I changed the first bulb at the bottom. Success! The bulbs must be burnt out and I was relieved it wasn't something more serious. While I'm at it, I might just as well change them all. One by one I changed them, and as the light penetrated the darkest corners of the basement, I could see Ed was right. 'There's a hell of a lot of work here.' I put the extra bulbs on a shelf near the stairs for easy access in case I needed them.

The furnace burning off and on that chilly autumn day wasn't enough to take away the damp, musty smell of the dirt floor and laid-up field stone walls in the basement.

I wanted to secure the outer basement door from the inside with the padlock I bought, but the inner door was swollen from the dampness and difficult to open. Taking a firm grip on the door handle, I braced my foot against the wall for leverage and gave it a stiff yank. The door cracked open slightly, just enough to get my hand behind it, and with a few more tugs, I forced it open the rest of the way, and was able to see the underside of the outside door.

The stairs were covered by cobwebs that gave the appearance of a fine curtain, suitable for a horror movie. My intrusion sent spiders running across their webs in every direction, ruining their nets used for catching the unwary flying insects. I found an old walking cane hanging on a pipe and brushed the remaining cobwebs away.

I'll put this new lock on the door just for added security, not that there's anything of value here yet to steal. Now that it's done, let me look at this old rusted electrical box. I laughed to myself, a 60 amp service with fuses, something that was done away with in the 1950s. Shaking my head in amazement, I closed the circuit box.

Tearing a piece of cardboard from an old box that was on a shelf, I put it on the dirt caked floor in front of the furnace. I wanted to kneel on it to get a better look inside the firebox. While I was on my hands and knees examining it, the furnace kicked on. With the sudden flash of light from the flame, I quickly drew my head back. 'What's that?' I thought.

Did I just see a shadow passing behind me? I quickly turned around, but there was nothing there.

That's the second time that happened, last night in the kitchen before I lit the kerosene lamp and down here today.

Getting back to examining the poor condition of the furnace and knowing I had to do something with the walls and floor, I realized it would have to be changed sooner than I previously thought. As I walked up the steps, I felt the same cool breeze cross my face, the breeze I felt examining the mystery closet with a window on the second floor. When I got to the kitchen, I closed the basement door, wondering what could be causing it. I knew old houses were drafty, but generally only in selective areas. When I turned, I was startled again. Frank was standing in the kitchen.

"I knocked but didn't get no answer. The front door was slightly open, so I just walked in. I thought you might be needin' a little help. Anything I can do?" he asked.

"No, I just looked over the furnace and electrical box. Both are pretty old and will have to be changed. Can you tell me when the furnace was converted from coal to oil heat? Do you remember?"

"Let's see now. If my memory's correct, it had to be about 60 years ago or more. I was still pretty young. I remember we used to carry the coal by bucket down the basement from the outside steps. We used to pile it in the corner where the oil tanks are now."

"Yeah, I saw a little still piled in the corner. I see some Mason jars on the shelves too. Were they your mothers?"

"They must have been. I didn't know there was any left downstairs. I guess when my sister helped her move 12 years ago, she musta' forgot them."

"Frank, when did your parents buy the house?"

"I was just a baby. I think it was 1946."

I was wondering if the money I found was something his parents saved, but the bills were in numerical order and dated 1932, so it wasn't likely. They must have been there from the previous owner and never discovered by Frank's family.

"I'm not going to do much more than the basics this weekend. It's just to get a rough idea of what has to be done and in what order I'm going to tackle it."

"Yeah, I saw the linoleum from upstairs piled in the dining room. It brings back memories from when I was little. We used to get out of bed on cold winter days, and our feet hitting that cold linoleum floor made you get dressed in a hell of a hurry. Sometimes we would run down and stand over the heater vent to get dressed."

I could relate to his words, remembering as a kid living in the city when we had a coal furnace. Although there was duct work in the basement there, it really didn't do much for the upper floors. Most of the heat came straight up through the grating to the first floor, and I'm sure with the absence of ductwork in the basement here, it was pretty much the same.

"Frank," I said changing the subject, "What was the room at the top of the stairs used for? It's too small to be a bedroom, and if it was a closet, why the window?"

Seemingly mulling that question, he replied, "For as long as I can remember, it's a room we never used for nothin' other than storage. I guess you noticed there ain't much closet space."

"I know what you mean about not much closet space. I'll have to do something about that."

We walked outside and across the road to the barn.

"What can you tell me about the barn?" I gestured at the building in front of us.

"I only know the barn was originally half the size it is now, and at the turn of the century, a barn down the road a hundred years younger was brought up and added to it. When they put the barns together, they left the wooden silo in the middle and fitted the new section right around it. Funniest thing you ever saw. Most people thought it was some sort of building mistake."

That explained to me why there were two sets of sliding doors on one side.

Frank continued. "When we were kids, me and my brothers would climb up in the silo and jump out into the hay pile," briefly smiling at the memory. "One thing I didn't like though, I didn't like going into the upper part of the barn alone. Especially on the side that was original."

"Why's that?"

"I thought it always felt a little cooler, even on hot summer days. Never knew why."

With him describing the same feeling I felt across my face in the house, I pried.

"What do you mean 'cooler'?"

"Not normal like the rest of the barn. One time when I was leading the plow horse through that section, the horse went completely wild and threw me on the floor. It wasn't normal, and that horse otherwise was mild as a kitten."

I was more interested in getting a better idea of why the roof of the old barn was sagging and only half heartedly listened to his story. After walking in, I saw the reason. Someone in the past had taken a few rafters out to make room for the half that was added. In doing so, they weakened the roof structure. With heavy snow in the winter, which is normal here, and the lack of maintenance probably since Frank's father passed away, water leaked in. The barn floor was at road level, and had a few soft spots. The sub-level walls below were made of field stone.

Frank remarked as he pointed down the stairs to the lower level, "That's where we kept our 17 dairy cows at one time," reminiscing as he looked around. "When I was younger, me and my brothers used to help with the milkin. It was all done by hand in those days. Washing milk cans, feeding and watering the live stock, raising hay, corn for feed. Too much work. Now everything's automation, all done by machine. We never really liked farming, seeing my mother and father always working so hard and only making enough to survive with just a little extra. We all found jobs doing something else."

What he told me about the barn section that seemed a little cooler even on warm days, intrigued me, but I put it in the back of my mind as we exited the barn.

Walking Frank to his truck, I remarked, "Oh! By the way, you were right about the good food at the Chatterbox. While I was there, a friend of yours introduced himself. I think his name was Ed. He seems like a real nice guy."

"Yeah, Ed and me, we go back a long way, all the way back to elementary school. He's the kind of guy you enjoy being around. He seemed to like getting into mischief." Laughing, he continued, "I think he'd tie a knot in the devil's tail just for a laugh."

As he was getting into his truck, he repeated again, "Well goodbye again. Remember, if you need anything, let me know."

As I watched him drive away, I thought to myself, 'He wouldn't only get to be a good neighbor, but a good friend as well.'

As I walked to the house, the sun was setting, and the sky was a bright, yellowish-orange color. With the tree shapes against the vibrant background, they looked like figures cut from black construction paper pasted to the setting sun.

I stood on the front porch for a few minutes admiring the view, then went in and locked the door. There wasn't much else to do, and I just sat in the kitchen listening to the radio drinking a cup of coffee, working on some figures of what the different projects would cost. At 9 o'clock, I was getting a little tired of working on the figures, and decided to take a shower and call it a night.

The bathroom was the better room in the house and wasn't in great shape by a long shot. I scoured the hell out of the tub during the afternoon, and felt it was clean enough to stand in and take a shower.

The walls were composition board for the tub lining, and from being water soaked at the bottom over the years, they were discolored and crumbling apart.

After doing the work I accomplished today and as dirty as I was, I wasn't getting into my sleeping bag without a shower. The warm water felt good running over my dirty body, but it was slow coming out of the shower head, so I increased the flow by turning the handle a little further. There must have been a fine line between warm and super hot. With the little extra turn, it felt like steam coming out. I jumped to one side to avoid getting scalded, but lost my balance and brought the shower curtain down, trying to break my fall. I was covered with soap, and decided the smart thing to do was test the water temperature first, before getting back in to rinse off.

My next thought was, 'I'll have to add new tub faucets to the top of my priority list for repairs.' The medicine cabinet was wood and looked like it was from the 1930s. The mirror had several large black spots where the silver paint behind the glass was worn off, and made it a little difficult to shave, having to move my head around the spots.

After my ordeal in the bathroom, I went out and got comfortable in my sleeping bag. I had been asleep for about an hour when a knock at the door woke me. I got up, stumbling to the door to answer it, and through the small window, I saw a man dressed in black with a black hat. I thought at first he was one of the Amish neighbors and opened the door. He was facing away from me and after I opened it, he quickly turned around. Startled, I was looking at the same man with the angry look that passed me the night I arrived.

I wasn't sure of his intentions and prepared myself for a possible confrontation, asking in a rough voice.

"Is there something I can do for you?"

He didn't seem to be angry with me, but had a look of bewilderment on his face.

"I'm looking for directions," he said.

Feeling almost sorry I confronted him so harshly, I replied, "I'm sorry, I'm new here and don't know many people. Are you looking for an Amish family?"

"No, I'm not Amish, I'm a Quaker. The land looks familiar, but the house, the barn and the people are different. I'm looking for my son. I know he was headed here."

"Where is he coming from? Maybe it's taking him longer than he expected."

"He's coming from the meeting at the church. The house that should be right here isn't here, and the barn's bigger than the one that's supposed to be there too."

I could see there was a woman in the carriage, and she looked like the same woman from the night before, staring straight ahead without expression. Seemingly puzzled, he kept looking around and continued. "I've been traveling up and down this road for a long time. I can't figure it out."

"I'm sorry I can't be more help. Maybe my neighbor Frank that lives down the road can help you."

As he turned and walked away, I closed the door. Through the small window of the front door, I watched as he walked off the porch, shaking his head walking back to the carriage. When I went to the front window to see which direction he was going, the carriage was gone. It had completely vanished. It couldn't be!

This was beginning to get a little on the weird side. No. Not a little, a lot on the weird side. I wondered whether it was a product of my own imagination or someone playing a trick on me. Maybe it was Frank and some of his pals giving me a housewarming and would be coming out from behind the house laughing. I waited- Nothing. I was wondering whether it was me or the area. I got back into my sleeping bag bewildered, trying to figure it out. Finally, I drifted off to sleep.

Chapter 5

During the night, the wind off the mountain picked up, and with the loose drafty windows rattling, it woke me out of my sleep. My eyes were only open for a few seconds when I thought I saw a shadow. What's that? It seems to be a shadow passing through the living room? I suddenly had an eerie feeling I wasn't alone. I rubbed my eyes to make sure, and with a closer look, yes! It's a figure of a woman moving through the living room. She had a long black dress and a split bonnet headpiece with a white rim, just like the woman in the carriage. It looked as though she wasn't walking, but seemed to be at a steady pace, sort of gliding across the floor. I sat up, and in a frightened loud voice called to her, "Hey! Who are you?" She seemed to ignore my statement, and I noticed as she passed by the front window, she seemed to be transparent. That really shook me out of my half-awake sleep. Sitting up, I realized she didn't seem to be aware of me being there, and I felt temporarily relieved that she wasn't focused on me.

She didn't seem to hear me as she went by, and without turning, headed straight for the stairs, paused- then went up. I managed to nervously unzip my sleeping bag and sit up, the whole time following her with my eyes. When she reached the landing, she turned and looked down at me as if she was just aware of my presence. With the landing window behind her, a full moon revealed she was transparent. Yes, the same as when she passed the window in the living room. Where was she going? I believed she would go to the left into the hall, but wait! She went to the right, into the closet with the window.

Quickly getting out of my sleeping bag, I apprehensively climbed the dark stairs trying to see if she was still there. When I got to the landing,

I cautiously cracked opened the door to the small room. I looked and for a moment thought I saw several bolts of cloth leaning up against the wall in one corner, something that wasn't there this afternoon. I was sure of it. Then, for a split second, I thought I heard a child crying and saw what looked like a toddler's leg sticking out from behind the bolts of cloth, as if he was sitting there playing hide-and-go seek. When I opened the door all the way, I saw the room was empty. How could this be? I felt a cool breeze go across my face again, as it did this afternoon and a chill slowly crept up my spine, causing the hairs on the back of my neck to rise. I had to pinch myself to feel if I was awake or dreaming. Sure enough when it hurt, I knew I was awake.

I quickly headed back down the stairs looking behind me as I went, making sure I wasn't being followed. I tried getting comfortable in my sleeping bag again, but without much success. I thought about what Frank told me about the barn and the three instances I had yesterday and again today in the basement. My mind was racing, trying to piece it all together. I lit the lamp again just as a precaution- precaution to what? I didn't know, but I wasn't taking any chances. Staring at the ceiling, I saw a spider making a web in the corner. Thinking about what I'd just experienced, it seemed like the right time of year for what transpired. Mysterious breezes crossing my face; spirits, spiders weaving webs, and scurrying across their silky creations in the basement. I thought, 'It's the right time of year for it- October.' Eventually being tired from working all day, sleep came over me once again.

I was happy to see the dawn and felt a little relieved with the sunlight flooding the room through the bare windows. Like a cleansing agent, it erased the darkness and things that go bump in the night, and the feeling that I wasn't really wanted here. The lamp was almost out of fuel from being lit all night, and the odor of the burning dry wick was strong. Getting out of my sleeping bag I looked up the steps again. Should I go up and check out the closet with the window? No, I think I'll pass until after breakfast. I was getting a little hungry and thought I would stop on the way to town and ask Frank a few questions.

As I passed his house, I saw him at his garage, looking at a bull-dozer he used for his business. I stopped and asked, "Frank, Think you want to go to breakfast with me?"

Walking toward me wiping the grease from his hands with a dirty rag he replied, "

"No, Ray. I really can't, too busy. Besides, June and I had breakfast a little while ago." Looking up making sure he wiped all the grease from his hands' he said, "Speak of the devil. Here she comes now."

Jokingly I asked loud enough for her to hear, "Ok. Frank! What was that? Who's the devil?"

"Shhh! This is June comin.' She's my wife."

I got out of the car to introduce myself. "Pleased to meet you- I'm your new neighbor Ray."

She replied giving Frank an evil look, "I'm the devil he just told you about, the one that made his breakfast this morning and just might not make it tomorrow morning."

It didn't take a long examination to understand they had a great sense of humor between them. June was short, about 5 feet tall, or a little more, wearing coveralls and a red plaid shirt with a red bandanna hold-ing back her light brown hair. She didn't look to be a person who would shy away from getting on a tractor if Frank for some reason wasn't able.

I grinned at her remark. Getting right to the point I asked, "Frank, did anyone in your family ever experience seeing any apparitions?"

Bringing his attention back to me he asked, "Apparitions?"

"Yeah, Ghosts."

He seemed bewildered at my question, staring at me for a few moments then looked at June inquisitively, as if he was taking a cue from her on whether to respond to my question. She seemed to have no objection to what I asked, and he began relating his sister's troubles.

"Well, just my sister Elizabeth. She used to have to spend almost the whole month of October with our aunt and uncle in town because of her experiences. Why?"

"Can you tell me about them?" I responded with an urgency that seemed to unsettle them both.

He raised the bill of his cap slightly settling it on the back of his head and thought for a moment.

"Let me see now. It first started when she was about nine."

June helpfully interrupted. "I think she was younger than that."

"Well, maybe she was eight. I don't rightly remember exactly. At first, mum and dad thought she was having hallucinations from some kind of a brain disorder, but after all the tests were negative, they decided to send her to my dad's sister. My Aunt Ethel lives in town, and they thought the change of scenery might help."

"Did it?"

"After she went, she didn't seem to have a problem. She came back home in November, and everything was fine- we thought it was over. Well sir, come next October, it happened again. And they shipped her off to Aunt Ethel's once more. In mid-November she came back, and everything was good again. October come the following year, the same thing. Hairs would rise up on the back of her neck. Something you could actually see, Scary!"

When he said that, he identified exactly the same sensation I felt during my experience last night, and I waited for him to tell me what she saw.

"How long did this go on?"

"Well, this went on until she was- oh, about 15 or so, then it didn't seem to bother her after that. Mum sort of thought it was her being a child and all, and just grew out of it."

I had to be careful here, because I really didn't know these folks well enough yet to share what I thought I saw in the house. Instead, I asked, "Was anyone else in your family affected?"

"No. Just her."

I decided to drop the questions. I didn't want to walk into the Chatterbox next weekend and have the place suddenly go quiet, knowing I was the topic of conversation for the entire week, being labeled the kook who sees ghosts. I thanked Frank for his input then turned to June. "It's a pleasure to meet you, Mrs. Devil__ err__ I mean June."

They both laughed as she gave Frank a poke in the ribs and a look of, 'You're going to be sitting on eggs this week. I'll get even with you somehow.'

As I got back in the car, I was wondering why they hadn't asked me why I wanted to know about apparitions and left heading for town. En route I asked myself a few questions. Why, out of everyone in his family only his sister had the problem, and why only this time of year? I also wondered why I was going to be so gifted with something I could do without.

The drive into town was as enjoyable as it was yesterday, with the window rolled down and the cool crisp air rushing in. 'This was real,' I thought. Not some ghostly woman gliding around my house.

I glanced in the rearview mirror and saw the dry leaves on the road being stirred up into a swirl as I drove over them. They were in abundance, being shed from the many trees overhanging the roadway.

The occasional whiff of hickory smoke seemed stronger than yesterday, escaping from smokehouses where farmers were preparing meats from animals they recently slaughtered. I thought, 'After I move here, would I be able to buy some from one of the farmers, or would I have to learn how to do it myself?' an interesting question.

When I arrived at the restaurant, being Saturday, there was more of a crowd than the day before. There were no tables available, so I took a seat at the counter and was promptly greeted by the waitress who had waited on me the day before. What was her name now? Oh, I remember! Ruthie.

"Are you making any headway clearing out the place?" she asked as she passed me coming from the kitchen holding a tray.

"Yes, I began taking up the old rugs and linoleum."

After she delivered the food tray she was carrying, she returned behind the counter. "I remember. You take regular coffee, right?"

"That's right."

After filling my coffee mug, she introduced the man sitting next to me.

She said, "I don't know whether you've already been introduced, but this is Dave. He lives just down the road from you a little piece. Dave, he's the flatlander that just bought the farm down the road from you. You know, Wilber and Lena's old place."

He smiled and said hello, extending his hand in friendship.

Although we were seated, Dave looked to be in his mid 40s, with salt and pepper hair and well over 6' feet tall.

"Are you moving in?" he asked, taking a sip of his hot coffee.

"No, I'll only be coming up on weekends to work on the place." pausing for a moment, "Dave, can I ask you a question?"

"Sure!"

Although the restaurant was busy, Ruthie stood there curious about the question I was about to ask.

"Did you ever experience seeing a horse and buggy passing your farm?"

He laughed, "I see them all the time. There are Amish carriages everywhere."

I told him about the one I saw the night I arrived, and how I was puzzled by the angry look on the driver's face as he passed. When I said, "The angry look on the drivers face," his laugh turned serious and I knew I struck something familiar. Why the change all of a sudden? Before I could ask, he repeated what must have been a familiar Halloween story amongst the townspeople replying,

"I knew Frank's sister had to move to her aunt's here in town in October." After taking another sip from his mug, he leaned toward me quietly saying, "One night when I was outside my barn, a horse and carriage passed me with a man that gave me an angry look like that. I thought he was Amish too, until one of the Amish men told me he couldn't have been Amish if he was clean shaven."

"Why not:" I asked.

"He explained to me that from the day Amish men marry, they don't shave. If he was clean shaven, chances are he was a Quaker. I don't know what else he could have been."

It felt good to talk to someone who experienced what I had, and the idea of it being in my imagination was finally laid to rest.

"A man dressed in black knocked on my door last night. He was the same man that passed me the first night I arrived, giving me an angry look as he went by the barn in his coach. I thought he was Amish too, but he explained to me he was a Quaker."

Leaning toward me trying not to be overheard, he seemed to become genuinely interested asking, "You actually spoke to him?"

"Yes, he knocked on my front door and seemed confused. He said the house and barn were different, but he was sure that where my house is, was where the house they were looking for was supposed to be."

Dave whispered, "Was there anyone else in the coach?"

"There was a woman sitting beside him. She was expressionless, staring straight ahead the same as the night before."

We were both silent for a few seconds, then I asked. "Can you remember what time of year it was when it happened to you?"

"It was in the fall," looking around as if he was about to reveal a secret he didn't want anyone else to hear, "About this time of year, October:"

After saying it, I noticed he seemed to be getting more uncomfortable in his seat as I related my story. It became obvious it was something he felt uncomfortable talking about.

"I have to leave," he said suddenly, taking a final gulp of coffee. "Nice talking to ya."

As Ruthie took my order, I realized Dave had not only skipped breakfast if it had been his intention, but his coffee mug was still half full and he didn't pay his check. She looked at his empty stool, then back at me, wondering why, but didn't say anything. I quickly ate my breakfast then quietly paid the tab for both of us. Saying goodbye to Ruthie, I put down the tip and left.

I was beginning to wonder where all this would lead and maybe struck on the real reason the previous owner sold so soon after buying it.

Chapter 6

I returned to the house and began trying to do something temporarily to repair the shower curtain I tore when I slipped trying to avoid the hot water the night before. I was still struggling to understand what the room upstairs which I now thought of as a windowed closet, and what it had to do with the apparition I had seen last night. I put it off long enough. As I walked up the steps, I could feel a chill going up my spine once again and the hairs on the back of my neck rise, and wondered whether all the conversation about spirits, were playing tricks with my mind. I opened the door but there was nothing unusual, other than the room seemed a little cooler. No crying sound of a toddler or bolts of cloth leaning in the corner that a child could hide behind.

The coolness of the room was the same description Frank gave me about the older side of the barn, and I thought I'd go across the road to see if I notice a difference. Entering the barn through the newer end, I slowly walked through to the older side. There were several soft spots in the floor where water seeping through the roof rotted the floor boards, and I had to be careful I didn't step on one- falling through to the lower section. The ropes and hand forged hooks used for hoisting the bales of hay into stacks were still hanging from the high ceiling and neatly coiled around wooden pegs extending from the support beams. Bales of unused hay were carefully stacked in one corner, and a few were haphazardly scattered around the floor, the only remnants remaining that identified it as a dairy farm.

As I passed the overhead beams that connected the two halves together, I noticed immediately. Yes! I'll be damned, there is a difference! The wind was blowing through the spaces where barn boards were missing, but the temperature should have been equal and not different. Like opening the door to the closet with the window, the hairs on the back of my neck rose again. I ran my hand over my head to the back of my neck, trying to settle them down, but without success. No good, even the warmth of my hand couldn't settle them down. This was crazy. I had to get out of there and couldn't exit the barn fast enough. I thought, 'Let me get out of here.' After exiting, the hairs laid down by themselves, and I felt relieved.

As I walked up the hill returning to the house, I stopped and looked back at the barn. I knew it was going to be torn down and that would eliminate one problem. The house was another matter, and I wondered whether I should do the same and assure myself both problems would be eliminated. I thought, 'Before I make that decision, I'll go through the house and make a mental note as to where the strongest feelings occur.'

I began exploring each room beginning at the second floor. Something I didn't feel when I originally went into the front bedroom changed. I was now feeling the hairs rising on my neck. The feelings weren't as strong as the windowed closet but they were definitely there. I went to the basement again but didn't feel anything. Walking through the rooms on the first floor, nothing! I tried concentrating on the bathroom. Nothing out of the ordinary there either, maybe it was only a malfunction of the plumbing.

The whole thing had taken over my mind, and I was at a loss trying to piece it all together. What did the freaky windowed closet in the house, the barn and the mysterious horse and carriage have in common? I couldn't understand but was determined to find out. If they were spirits that couldn't find peace, I wanted to know why. And why it was always October that they were seen.

After settling comfortably in my sleeping bag, I couldn't put my mind to rest. I became suspicious of every sound, and my hearing suddenly became more acute. Unless I stopped imagining there was a threat with every noise, I realized I would never get to sleep. Several times during the night I awoke, and looked around just to make sure I was still alone before closing my eyes again. On one occasion I looked at my watch and saw it was only 3:30. Wait! Do I smell wood burning? I quickly unzipped my sleeping bag and sat up. The kerosene lamp wasn't lit, and besides, it's a completely different odor. This was definitely the smell of wood burning. After looking in the basement to assure myself there wasn't a problem, I returned to my sleeping bag. I thought, 'Maybe the wind is blowing smoke from someone's wood burning stove. Wait a minute! The nearest neighbor is a quarter mile away. I know the house is modern and he would more than likely use oil for heating the same as me, so that couldn't be it.' Knowing it wasn't something going on in the house I was satisfied, and fell back to asleep.

After waking I quickly brushed my teeth. Knowing I had to leave early, I had already gathered my dirty laundry and placed it by the front door. After loading the car, I locked the front door and started back to the city. Driving down the hill I looked back and imagined my household of spirits, gathered at the front window toasting my departure.

Just before hitting the turnpike, I stopped for a coffee to go before heading south on the last leg of my journey.

I relaxed and thought about my best friend Don and his wife Delores, and the talent she possesses. Hmmm- *Possesses!* Yes, *possesses*. That's right, Delores is a psychic. Maybe she can cast some light on my problem. I wonder if they would take a trip up with me.

My mind wandered back to how Don and Delores became my best friends. They met through a female friend of mine on a double date and have been married for the past seven years. I also stood as his best man for his wedding. My relationship with Don goes back even before he was married, when we were in the same class at night school. We were both taking the same business courses trying to increase our resume. After we graduated, we both acquired jobs at Keystone. After working there for several years, Don decided to take another job offer with another company, but we never lost contact with each other.

Through spending so much time together, we realized we had a lot in common, pretty much sharing the same likes and dislikes. We enjoyed fishing, as well as going to baseball, and football games together.

Don, more than me, was a more enthusiastic football fan and seldom missed going to a Philadelphia Eagles home game. We were season ticket holders. Every Sunday home game- rain, freezing temperatures and occasionally snow, we were present. Don would wear his Eagles hat and sweatshirt, and wear his throat raw, yelling at a bad call from the referees, or cheering a large gain in yardage. Sometimes, he would yell until his voice broke, and I'd have to calm him down, so people with seats around us could enjoy the game.

Some of the fans around us were season ticket holders also, and like us, had the same seats every year. They were used to his outbursts and sometime were more interested in his reaction to a call than the game itself. They often goaded him, pretending to sympathize with a bad call from the referee, and that would only rile him a little more, especially if the Eagles weren't performing well.

After the game, we usually stopped at Paul's Steaks in South Philly for a few sandwiches to go then wound up at my apartment for a few beers, to re-hash the highlights-and lowlights-of the game. By then, he would be calmed down and the beer always served as a soothing agent for his much irritated throat.

Don's wife__ Delores; was especially tolerant of our absence almost every Sunday afternoon during football season. We would gather with a few other friends at my apartment to watch football or go to a sports bar to watch the Eagles play their away games. She was also a pretty good sport about our overnight fishing trips.

If you didn't know them, seeing them standing next to each other was kind of comical. Don's over 6' feet, and Delores is about 5 feet one inch-a real "Mutt and Jeff" combination. In spite of their physical differences, they complemented each other by sharing the same interests and dislikes.

She's an attractive, well built woman in her early 30s with unique facial features. Her long black hair, full lips and high cheek bones made her look almost goddess-like, and I was sure her lineage was possibly from the area of Romania.

Yes, there's no doubt about it. She's beautiful. A woman like that would be every man's dream, and I had to choose the tall blond I was married to. Then again, I saw Delores as proof that there was someone still out there who would be a match for me, and that was comforting.

Delores also possesses another unique ability. I had heard from Don something I hadn't yet personally confirmed. Something she inherited, a talent from her mother and grandmother before her. As I understand from my conversations with him, her ability was with psychic powers. The talent; or ability- for lack of a better word, was being able to somehow strangely predict the future or communicate with spirits from the past. What she was capable of doing was hard to imagine, and most professionals would classify anyone who admits to such powers, a lunatic. And yet, I know Delores to be down to earth and far from being eccentric.

Don told me it started when she would give palm readings as a form of entertainment at parties they attended. Someone, inevitably hearing of her talent, would always ask for a reading. Several people who were read would leave laughing at the remotest chance of her predictions ever being fulfilled. When several people returned telling her about the uncanny accuracy of her predictions, they would ask for a second reading. She began to realize her ability was far and above her sister's and mother's talent and she began to get more and more calls for readings.

Her talent entered a whole new realm when a homicide detective from Camden, New Jersey called.

Delores vaguely recalled doing a reading for the wife of a police detective from Camden, a city across the Delaware River from Philadelphia. The caller asked if she was Delores Lee and identified himself as Camden Homicide Detective David Jones. Her initial reaction was one of alarm and asked franticly if anything had happened to Don. Psychics don't always know what lies ahead for them or their loved ones, which explained her reaction to the call. After reassuring her that he wasn't the bearer of bad news, he stumbled ahead with his reason for calling.

"If you'll just bare with me for a few minutes, I don't quite know how to start this conversation. It's not the everyday question anyone would ask."

After reassuring him that she was accustomed to hearing all sorts of requests and wouldn't pass judgment, she gained his trust encouraging him to continue.

He began, "Maybe I should start at the beginning. My wife went to a reading with you last year. You told her she would have to have a minor surgery within the next few weeks for something that couldn't wait. When she came home and told me, we both laughed. She had just gone through a complete physical and passed with flying colors. Two weeks later we were at the pool where we swim three nights a week, and she started experiencing tightness in her chest. Remembering what you told her, she insisted we drive straight to the hospital, something that was very unusual for my wife. Normally she passes off any small ache or pain. Luckily we did, after giving her a cardiogram, she was rushed to the operating room and immediately had a stent put in. She had a 98 percent blockage of her right coronary artery.

The doctor said if she would have gone home first, there would have been no guarantee she would have made it back to the hospital alive."

"Is she okay?" Delores frantically asked.

"Yes, thanks to you. She went back again several months ago, and you told her about her sister losing her husband. Thinking it was absurd and so remote, they too were in good shape physically, and enjoyed all sorts of sports activities. That is, until she went home to find a note that he'd left her for another woman. I guess she wished you were a little more specific as to how he was going to leave."

"I remember your wife now. She came here with two other women. She wasn't supposed to be read, but her friends insisted, and she had me read her too."

"That's right: Well, getting back to the reason I called. Have you ever been able to see or feel surroundings by holding a piece of clothing or an article a person owned?"

"I'm not sure I quite follow your question. Are you asking me to help on an investigation?"

"Yes, that's about what I'm trying to ask. If you feel you can give us some time where we can get together, I'd really appreciate it."

"Where do you want to meet me?"

"I could come to you, or you can come to the Camden City police headquarters, Homicide Unit, and ask for me, Detective David Jones. Here, it would be a much more controlled environment with witnesses. When can I make the appointment?"

"Tomorrow will be fine. I'll be there at 3:00 in the afternoon. My husband Don can drive me."

"That's great! I'm looking forward to meeting you."

According to Don, the next day when Delores arrived, they put her in a room equipped with a two-way mirror. There were two chairs and a table in the small room, with Detective Jones on one side and Delores on the other. A tape recorder was on the table with a microphone that he switched on as soon as she sat down, wanting to record everything that was said. He began by asking her name and a few other formalities for the record.

He took a partially blood-stained shirt from a brown bag that had a label attached to it with the word *"evidence"* marked boldly across the front. The shirt was small and looked like the style and colors of a parochial school blouse Delores guessed, possibly from a fifth or sixth grader.

"Have you ever held an article like this and had a vision, or feeling of the person that owned it, or however way you would put it?"

"Is this a piece of clothing from a homicide?" she asked.

"Not yet. Right now, she's just a missing person, but we suspect it will be if we can find the body. You're probably the last hope we have. The kid's been missing since school began in September."

"Let me hold the garment, I'll let you know what I feel."

Don explained how Jones handed her the garment, and she closed her eyes going into a semi-conscious state. Gently holding the shirt running her fingers over the fabric, she began to speak.

"I see a vacant lot with a rusted set of railroad tracks and weeds growing up around them. It's leading into the rear of a vacant building.

Yes, I can see it. It's an abandoned factory, a factory with a lot of broken windows high on the wall. The wall has graffiti on most of it, but the word *KING* is predominantly spray-painted in black, with a crown roughly drawn over it; large letters, very large letters."

She paused for a few more moments, as if she was personally standing there surveying the scene, then continued. "There's wooden pallets scattered around, and one propped up against a cyclone fence, holding it open. There are a few metal drums painted blue scattered around, with a few lying on their sides, and a few standing upright. I get a strong sensation for what I'm feeling right there."

Within a few minutes, she broke her concentration, and Detective Jones slowly turned off the recorder. Looking surprised, he reverently took back the garment, returning it to the bag.

"Are you aware of what you described?" he asked.

"No, I never know what I've said. But there is a strong presence connected to that garment of whatever I described. Who did it belong to?"

"It belonged to a little girl that's been missing since the first week of school. That's all the lead we have. It was found about two blocks from her home."

"That's tragic. I've never experienced anything like this before, it wasn't easy."

"I'm sure it wasn't. Thanks for your cooperation. Your husband is waiting in the lobby."

I remember asking Don if it helped, and him telling me one of the detectives remembered an old abandoned factory she had to pass on her way to school. When they investigated the rear of the factory, the first thing that stood out was the graffiti spray painted on the factory wall. They stopped and stood in amazement at the large spray-painted crown with the word *KING* written under it, exactly as Delores described. Looking at each other with a reassuring eye, they sensed something that was very unique from all their other investigations. They surveyed the lot with the railroad tracks leading into the back of the factory. After taking a series of photos, they called for more police to help with the search.

One of the officers checking the metal drums, found her remains inside one of them.

I remember him telling me the detective who did the interview called her to share how accurate she had been with describing the area behind the factory. He told her how skeptical he was about the process, but after seeing the results, he became a true believer. He was so taken by her success he asked if she could possibly aid them in a description, if she could by going to the site. Hesitant to agree because of her reaction to feeling the garment, she decided for the childes sake, it was the right thing to do.

After accompanying the detectives to the location behind the factory, without telling her where the body was found, she walked the vacant lot stopping close to where the metal drum that held the body had been. Closing her eyes, she told them the murder didn't take place here. It took place in a house.

She felt it was done by an older man who looks to be in his mid 50s, heavy set, with a bald head. That's all she could tell them.

I asked Don if they ever found the murderer, and he told me it was a neighbor who lived several houses away. He had a prior record of contributing to the delinquency of a minor, and when they searched his home, they found several articles of clothing that belonged to the deceased.

I asked him if Delores had done anything else for the police department, and he told me she had, once in a small New Jersey township, and another in Camden. From what he told me, he didn't care for her ability and mentioned to me on several occasions that he spoke to her about his concerns. He explained that after she comes out of her trance she seems exhausted for several hours, and sometimes even longer. I personally never saw her power demonstrated, but with her psychic ability, maybe she can help shed some light on my dilemma, and I wondered if Don and Delores would accompany me there next weekend.

With the skyline of the city coming into view, I was anxious to get to my apartment to make the call.

Chapter 7

After dialing the number, Don answered the phone.

"Hello, Don. I called to see if we could get together sometime during the week."

"I don't see any problem with it, how about Wednesday? You can come over for dinner. How was the weekend at the farm, were you able to get a lot accomplished?"

"That's what I'd like to talk to you and Delores about. It's been a weird weekend, to say the least."

"When we last spoke, you sounded like you were looking forward to getting away__ what happened?"

"I was anxious until I got to the farm. I had a few unwanted visitors."

Laughing, he said, "What do you mean unwanted visitors? Did the locals protest your buying the place? Did they congregate outside with signs? No more city slickers or pickets saying, 'Flatlanders go home'?"

"No. Nothing that subtle, the visitors I had were transparent and downright angry."

"What! What the hell are you talking about?" he exclaimed.

"Don: I think I bought a house that still has some restless spirits occupying it."

"Wait a minute. Are you trying to tell me the place has ghosts? It's haunted?"

"That's about the size of it. Shook the hell out of me I'll tell ya."

After giving him a brief rundown of my experiences, we agreed on me coming over for dinner on Wednesday evening after work.

"I'll see you then." Don remarked.

Hanging up the phone, I took the soiled clothes I was wearing at the farm and dumped them in the washer. It had only taken a few minutes when the phone rang. It was Delores excitedly asking, "What's this about spirits at your farm?"

I began telling her about my experiences over the weekend, when she abruptly interrupted. "Don't wait until Wednesday. If you're not busy, come over now. We're not doing anything."

I decided to go now and speak with them face-to-face, while it was all still fresh in my mind. When I got to their house they had already set out a few chips and some onion dip anticipating my arrival. Sitting in the living room, I began to relate my story of the weekend. Don looked a little skeptical, but Delores seemed to be absorbing every word like a sponge and was very attentive.

After I finished the narrative I asked, "Delores, have you ever been involved with or heard of anyone having a similar experience?"

"I have. In fact, it was here in the city. Coincidently, the apparition was also Quaker."

"When and where was that?" I asked.

"It happened to the Sullivan family. They lived in an old section of the city called Frankford. Their little girl Mary, as I recall, about the age of nine was in her living room when she saw a woman dressed in black come in through the front door, then go up the steps to the second floor. She described the woman as elderly, but you know kids, anyone taller than them they consider old. I distinctly remember her saying 'The woman seemed to glide across the floor, like Casper the Friendly Ghost.' a cartoon character she watches on TV."

"You said the woman came through the front door? You mean she opened the door or actually came through the front door?"

"Yes! She didn't open it the way we would. It was explained to me, when Mary felt the hair rise on the back of her neck she looked toward the door. She said there seemed to be a mist coming through it. As the mist got bigger, the woman came out of it. Mary followed her asking who she was and where she was going, but the woman never turned around or answered her. She described it the same way you did when the woman passed you during the night, as if the apparition wasn't aware of your presence."

It sounded very familiar with my experience, and when Delores said it, I could feel the hair on the back of my neck rise, just as it did Saturday night.

She continued. "According to Mary's mother, the spirit walked into a bedroom. Mary followed her, but when she opened the bedroom door, there was no one in the room. It seemed that Mary's sightings were on days when she sensed something different in the air. I took her to mean a certain amount of static electricity."

Listening to Delores, it sounded like the same way Frank described his sister Elizabeth's experiences.

She continued, "Mary's older brother Tommy on two occasions, saw a man and a woman both dressed in black enter the house and go straight through to the kitchen. He too called to them, but he didn't think they knew he was there. When he went to the kitchen, they had disappeared. After Tommy's second sighting, he went to the Frankford Historical Society, a building in the neighborhood to look at old maps of the area."

I was familiar with the Frankford section of the city, and knew it was settled in the late 1600s and had a ton of history attached to it. I also knew the early settlers were indeed Quakers.

"On one map, Tommy saw what looked like a cabin or a farm house in the exact location of his current row home."

"What, if anything, did they do about it?" I asked.

"They wound up living with the problem. Since they didn't think they were a threat, they figured they could co-exist. Tommy said it was kind of cool living with ghosts."

"Are they always just something in another dimension that couldn't harm you?" I asked.

"On the contrary, it depends on the way they died and what they're trying to free themselves from.

I personally feel that deaths that were premature from an accident or murder were spirits trying to free themselves from that time it took place, or correct circumstances that could have prevented it."

"That sounds logical. What about the temperature difference where the sightings took place?"

"That's normal. I experienced a wide range of temperature differences between hot and cold."

When she said hot, I immediately thought of the extreme temperature change that night taking a shower and about the angry look on the Quaker's face when he passed me. Could he have been the cause of it? Listening to her really had my brain in full gear. Was this the real reason the previous owner was reluctant to talk about the house at settlement? Did he have some sort of violent experience as I had with the hot water? All that was circulating in my mind the whole time I was listening and asked, "Although they're spirits, can they have the ability to move things that are real or something we can touch?"

"What do you mean by that?" she asked.

"I was just thinking. Friday night when I was in the shower, I turned the hot water faucet slightly to make the water warmer. I only turned it slightly, but it seemed like it went from warm to extremely hot. I had to literally jump out of the way to keep from getting scalded."

After what looked like a few moments of thought she replied, "Then your manifestations may be harmful.

If you're going back by yourself during the week, I'd use caution until we can figure out why they're so restless."

"You said 'we'. Do you mean that literally?"

"Hell yes! You didn't think I'd just sit here listening and not want to get involved, do you? When are you going back?"

"I guess you realize you already answered the question I was going to ask. I'm going to try and go back this Friday if I can get the day off again."

With what she said, I was beginning to realize maybe these events were on purpose, and the spirits I inherited with the house weren't harmless, as Delores suggested. With her help, I'd like to see if I can find out more about these spirits. Don sat silent during our discussion and I think by the look on his face, he would have liked the opportunity to make an excuse to be busy.

Delores enthusiastically exclaimed, "What time will you pick us up?"

"How about 10 o'clock? I was thinking about staying a few extra hours every day and getting ahead of my work. If I'm caught up, there's no reason why my boss wouldn't let me take off this Friday again. After listening to you, I absolutely have to try and get a handle on this thing."

"Why 10 o'clock: why so late?" she asked.

"Ok! How about you telling me, when should I pick you up?"

"We'll be ready at 8 o'clock, if that's ok with you?"

"Fine, I'll see you then."

I was happy she wanted to leave earlier, and the real reason I said 10, was not to impose on their already generous offer to go.

After saying goodnight I returned to my apartment. I had some contracts at home I could work on just to get ahead of things at the office, and began delving into the small details of the contracts. Before I realized it, when I glanced at the clock, it was already past 11:00. I told myself, 'There, that's finished. I'll be well ahead of things at the office.' Preparing for bed, I began rehashing my conversation with Delores. Brushing my teeth, I began to laugh thinking about Don's facial reaction to being involuntarily volunteered. Glancing up in the bathroom mirror I said, "Boo!" Writing the word on the steam covered mirror, and taking the conversation out of my mind for the rest of the night, I went to bed.

All week as hard as I tried, I couldn't keep from thinking about the spirits at the farm. They kept invading my mind and I had to fight back the thought so it wouldn't interrupt my work. I stayed late every day to get contracts finished, and on Thursday asked my boss Mr. Johnson, if I could take off again on Friday.

"Did you take care of the policy from last Thursday? I tried to get you before you left the office," he asked.

"Yes, I did Mr. Johnson. I saw your note and called Mr. Lawrence first thing Monday morning. I worked on a policy with him before. He remembered me and welcomed my services again."

"I thought you wrote a policy for him. That's why I wanted you to handle it."

"I just finished, it's on your desk for approval."

"You're a valuable asset to the company Ray. As long as you're on top of everything, I can't see any reason to deny you."

"Thanks Mr. Johnson. I'll see you Monday."

Early Friday morning, I drove to Don's house to pick them up. When I pulled onto their street, I saw them anxiously waiting at the curb.

As I pulled to the curb Don said, "Good morning Ray. I see you didn't have any problem getting off work."

"No, I wrote a few big policies this week. They're happy about that."

"Is old Mr. Johnson still your boss?" he asked.

"Yes, he's due to retire soon. I don't know who'll take over, but I have a strong suspicion he's grooming me as his replacement."

"I remember Mr. Johnson from when I worked there, he's a good egg. The company's going to miss his services. Does he still wear a bow tie?"

"Yes, he still wears a bowtie, and you're right- They're really going to miss his services. He mentioned to me he's thinking about relocating to Florida after he retires. Since his wife died several years ago, and he doesn't have any relatives, I think that's a good move on his part."

"Yeah, he didn't have children," Don replied.

I helped load their bags in the trunk, then headed out hitting the turnpike north, talking about my experience pretty much all the way to where we exit.

On the way, Delores questioned me about what the farm looked like and why I bought it.

"Look, Delores, staying overnight at the farm is out of the question. There's too much work to be done, and I don't have furniture to accommodate sleeping. It would be alright for a man like me or Don to rough it, but not for a woman."

Don replied, "Sorry to disappoint you Ray, but I don't want to stay there either."

Delores looked disappointed, but hearing me say I didn't have any sleeping accommodations didn't fight the issue.

"How were you able to stay there overnight?" she asked.

"I have my sleeping bag. I roll it open on the couch. It's fine. There's a Comfort Inn close by. We'll check in there and make the 17- mile trip to the farm every day."

Don seemed more relieved than Delores. Her interest in the psychic world took preference over everything else in her life, even her own comfort. I guess dealing with different spiritual situations made her more callous and less afraid of spirits. Where, on the other hand, Don was less afraid of spirits, especially the ones that read, 'Johnny Walker Red or Johnny Walker Black Scotch.' Driving through the Poconos, it was colorful with the autumn leaves and we finally arrived at the Comfort Inn in Wysox, a small town just outside the city of Towanda.

Chapter 8

After checking in, we unloaded our bags into adjoining rooms. A few minutes after putting my bags down, there was a knock at the door.

"Hey Ray, are you ready to eat? I'm kind of hungry," Don said.

I replied, "There's a small restaurant in town near where I live. We could have lunch there, unless you're hungry now and don't want to wait."

Delores replied instantly, "We'll wait; I'm enjoying the trip. The fall colors are beautiful, they haven't quite changed in the city yet."

As Don closed the door, I could hear him grumbling in a low but audible tone. "Thanks a lot answering for me Delores about postponing lunch, but I'm hungry now," he continued in a louder tone, "We passed a few nice restaurants right here in town," She ignored him as we walked to the car.

I commented, "Delores, up here, the leaves turn color earlier. Sometimes with an early snow, they'd be almost all gone by now. The people that live up here have a funny saying: 'You have to buy a Halloween Costume big enough to fit over a snow suit.'

She laughed as we headed out for Canton. The 17-mile drive to the farm passes through two small enclaves of houses, not really big enough to be considered a town.

The houses are a smattering of designs from different periods in the past, between the late 1700s, a few built right after the Civil War, and a few Victorian homes, quite an expanse of time.

Pointing to one, I asked, "Do you see that style house?"

"Yes: Why?" Don asked.

"The design is called French Federalist. They were built for those that were able to escape the guillotine during the French Revolution. Some of the houses have been added to since then, but they're still distinguishable from the newer homes. There's even an area here called French Azilum. It was set aside for Marie Antoinette and her entourage, but she never escaped. The area's now a historical site."

Delores replied, "I guess that's the reason there are so many French names. I noticed as we passed through them. La Plume, Wysox, Leroy, Laporte, they're all very French."

I turned off the main road onto the dirt road leading to the farm.

"Is this the road the farm's on?" Don asked.

"Yes."

As we approached Frank's house, he remarked, "Is this it?"

"No, that's where my neighbor Frank and his wife June live. That's my house and barn at the top of the hill."

The grade uphill is a little steeper, and at the top I pulled up in front of the barn.

"So, this is it?" Getting out of the car, Don looked back down the hill at the dust still settling from the dirt road. "You better be prepared to do a lot of car washing."

"I know Don. I didn't say living in the country was perfect, but I think the positives outweigh the negatives."

As we walked up the front lawn from the barn, they were taking in the panorama of the countryside. Delores seemed to enjoy the view.

"Look, Don! You can see across the valley. Those farms on that distant hill must be two miles away."

"Yeah Ray, you're right. It does have a hell of a view. Why don't we get lunch before looking at the inside of the house?" he suggested.

"I think that's a good idea."

Returning to the car, we drove to the Chatterbox for a late lunch. Most of the crowd was already gone, and finding an empty table wasn't a problem. After sitting down, Ruthie who served me twice before, came to our table handing us menus.

After Delores opened it, she quickly closed it again. Laughing, she said, "The cost of what all three of us will eat wouldn't buy one meal in Philadelphia."

The waitress, hearing what she said replied with a smile__ "Expensive, ain't it?" then took our order.

"I can't get over this menu. A full breakfast for six bucks, that's a real scream."

"Yes, I know. It's the same thing I thought when I looked at it. The bread's homemade too. So, what do you think of the property without being able to judge the inside?"

Don said, "I like the lay of the land with the cleared fields and the wooded mountain as the backdrop. I know whatever condition the house is in, with what you know about working with tools, the place would be habitable in no time. But I'll reserve my full opinion until I get a chance to see the inside."

When Ruthie returned with our food she asked, "Are these friends from the city to help you with the work?"

"No Ruthie, they're just friends I'm showing the property to."

"So you remembered my name huh?" she replied before continuing, "Makes me feel real important!"

Turning to Delores and Don she said, "Pleased to meet ya! Hope you enjoy your lunch."

"Thanks, I'm sure we will." Delores replied.

Ed, Frank's friend from the coffee clutch approached our table.

"Hello Ray, is this a work party?"

"No Ed, just friends visiting."

Don stood up and shook his hand. "Nice country you have here."

"Yeah, we like it!" Ed replied, "Ray, I saw Frank this past week. He told me you mentioned my name."

"Yes, I told him you introduced yourself to me."

"Yeah, me and Frank go back, oh; about 60 years. We went to school together. Well, nice meetin' you folks." as he headed for the door.

After he walked away, Delores looked at me remarking, "It didn't take you long to start knowing people."

"No, that's life in a small town."

Still amused at the menu, she kept commenting on it.

After finishing our meal we drove back to the farm. When we pulled up in front of the barn, Delores said, "I want to go inside and examine it first."

Without telling her which section of the barn was older, she entered the newer section with Don and me following.

"Be careful where you're stepping," I told them, "A few of the floor boards are soft. I wouldn't want you to fall through."

Walking carefully looking at the floor, she was about to pass through to the older side, then suddenly hesitated.

"I feel an immediate change in temperature right here."

I guess I was right, she sensed the same thing I had. I never mentioned where the barns came together, but she stopped at the exact spot. The spot where I felt the temperature change when the hairs on the back of my neck rose. Continuing through she exited the side of the barn where my car was parked. We walked up the front lawn to the porch and I took out the keys for the front door.

Unlocking it, I pushed it open, Delores immediately stepped back.

"What's wrong?" I asked, "Is the place that much of a shock?"

"No, but when you opened the door, I felt an immediate presence. Even before I stepped inside."

After going in the house, it was a little chilly from me having the thermostat turned down in my absence all week. I went to the dining room and raised the temperature to 72 degrees and the heater kicked on. After closing the door, I took them on a tour of the house.

Don looked around and said, "Ray, I've seen some piss-poor properties you fixed up before like that duplex, but this place has that beat by a mile. This has to be one of the most challenging I've ever seen. I could never see your ex living here."

Replying, "I know, and to quote the waitress that served us lunch the first day I met her, 'Maybe that's why she's an ex.'" they laughed.

"It seems like everyone up here don't have any trouble speaking their mind." Delores commented.

"That's for sure."

When we reached the landing on the second floor, I pointed out the windowed closet to Delores. "This is where I saw the apparition of the woman go. The image of a toddler's leg was sticking out from behind several bolts of cloth that were leaning against the wall in that corner," pointing to it.

She laughed at my description of the closet with a window.

"Why the laughter, do you know something I don't?"

Still chuckling she answered, "It's probably a sewing room. It's a place where the woman of the house could recluse herself and make or mend clothing. That's the reason for its small size and the window. The room didn't have to be that big, and the window was for sunlight so she could see what she was working on. It could also be the reason you saw the bolts of cloth."

I laughed to myself thinking, 'I'm not so stupid, Frank's family lived here for 40 plus years and didn't know its purpose.'

"Why is it much cooler upstairs, is it a gathering of ghosts?" Don asked.

Delores looked at him, not enjoying the idea that he seemed to be mocking my dilemma.

"No Don, in old houses there was only one source of heat. It was probably a wood burning stove centrally located downstairs. The oven for the kitchen would be the same and heat on the second floor was strictly gravity controlled."

As we walked through the bedrooms, Don asked, "What are you going to do for heat upstairs?"

"I'm going to put individual electric baseboard radiators with separate controls in each room instead of all the trouble with running duct work."

Delores seemed to be annoyed at our delay wanting to examine the rest of the house. Cutting our conversation short she said, "I'd like to look in the basement now Ray, I want to see if I feel any reaction."

Going back down the steps I could hear the old furnace clanking, making noise putting out a little heat. We went to the kitchen, and I suddenly remembered my friend the rat. I thought, 'I hope when I open this basement door he isn't staring us in the face to embarrass me.' Slowly opening it, I peered into the darkness of the landing. To my relief, he wasn't there.

As we were going down the stairs, the light bulb I had replaced at the bottom of the steps only the week before, grew brighter with intensity far beyond its capability of 60 watts, then seemed to explode.

"That's strange Ray. I've seen bulbs burn out, but never saw a light bulb turn that brilliant, then burst like that." Don remarked.

Stopping momentarily, I used my flashlight to guide our way safely down the rest of the steps. Finding the light bulbs I purchased the week before, I replaced the one that burst.

"They must be cheap bulbs," Don suggested.

"Maybe: There, that one works. Let's see how long it lasts."

"Ray, where did you see the shadow passing behind you?" Delores asked.

"Right here in front of the furnace. There's the cardboard I was kneeling on. I saw the shadow come from that direction where the shelves are. It passed behind me."

Walking slowly over to the shelves, she paused for a moment, closing her eyes. After a few moments she said, "I don't feel anything right here."

I felt discouraged but the examination wasn't complete. I opened the door to the stairs that led to the outside showing her the stone with the name "Smythe 1742" inscribed on it. She reverently touched the stone and closed her eyes obviously trying to feel any psychic connection. She didn't say anything, but by the look she gave me, it told me she seemed to know more than what she was revealing. Although she kept silent, I was happy there seemed to be some reaction on her part. Whether it was good or bad, I didn't know, but it was something we could try to deal with.

Scanning the room, Don shook his head again at the site of the old furnace and the dirt-caked floor. Before going up the stairs, he said, "This is going to be one hell of a major project in itself."

Going back to the kitchen, I brewed a pot of coffee. We sat down at the kitchen table and I asked, "Well Delores, now that you examined it, what are your thoughts?"

Looking down at her coffee cup then slowly up at me without saying anything, I took it her hesitancy was due to gathering her thoughts on how to put her feelings. Seeing the anxiousness for an answer on my part she replied, "There's definitely a connection with the stone and the occupants, but I'm a little confused with the connection with the older portion of the barn. You said that part is from a different period. What did you mean?"

"Frank told me the older section where you felt the temperature difference had been here. The newer section is about a hundred years younger. It was brought up from another farm down the road.

Did you feel anything upstairs in the sewing room?"

"I felt an urgency of a spirit trying to help someone, probably a member of the family, but from what? I couldn't speculate. We'll have to wait and see if they'll communicate with us later."

"What do you mean communicate with us later, you mean a séance?

"Yes, that's the only way you can communicate with spirits. We'll need a fourth person to have one though. I know you're new here. Do you have anyone you could ask that would be interested__ maybe Frank or his wife?"

"I don't know. I'm sort of embarrassed to ask. I haven't known them that long. Maybe they'll think I'm crazy, or we're going to start some kind of cult here."

"Well, you told me his sister had problems. Maybe he'll be sympathetic. You said they were real nice people."

"Yes they are."

"Good! Why don't you ask?"

"Ok, make yourself comfortable," I smiled, gesturing to an empty room. "I'll be right back."

I drove down the road and found Frank working on his heavy equipment where I had seen him most of the time. As I pulled into his driveway, he looked up from the motor of his truck and walked toward me.

"Hi Ray, I noticed you have company this weekend, they here to help?"

I cut right to the chase, "Frank my friend's wife's here. She wants to have a séance and we need a fourth person. Would you or June be interested?"

Looking at me a little skeptical replied, "I don't think I want to be there, but why go through all the trouble? I told you before, only my sister felt their presence, and even that stopped after she was about 15."

"Well, I hate to tell you, but I'm feeling the same presence, and I'm older than 15, I just want to try to get rid of them if it's possible. Do you know anyone else that might be interested?"

He raised and lowered the bill on his baseball cap several times, as he had done when I asked him questions before. I thought to myself, 'It must be the starting up of his thought process, like a starter on one of his heavy bulldozers."

Straightening his cap again, he replied, "There's old George. He might do it. He's the local dowser."

"Ok, that's a new one on me. What's a dowser?" I asked.

"He finds water that's under the ground for people who want to drill for a well. You know; a water witch."

Now it was my turn to be skeptical. "How does he do that?"

"He takes a forked stick and walks around the ground where you want a well- When he walks over an underground spring, the branch points down to the ground."

I looked at him with raised eyebrows but hearing this for the first time, I didn't dismiss his statement asking, "Do you think he'd be willing to do it?"

Settling his cap back on his head, and a shrug of his shoulders replied,

"No harm in askin'. I'll show you where he lives. Just let me wipe some of the grease off my hands, I don't want to dirty up your car."

Grabbing a clean rag, he wiped his hands then got in giving me directions to George's farm. It wasn't far, about three miles.

When we pulled up in the driveway, there was an old man sitting in a chair on the back porch. Exactly what one would expect, if you had to guess what a water witch looked like.

"There he is."

"How old is he?" I asked.

"I think George is about 90 or so."

He was separating apples from a basket, obviously from the three trees in his yard, and there were still quite a few on them and a lot still on the ground. Not recognizing the car he stood up. When he saw us walking up the stone path toward him, he recognized Frank.

"Hello, Frank! I didn't recognize the car. I haven't seen you in a long time. Where you been hidin'?"

"Well: ya know, I been pretty busy. I see you have a job cut out for you with all those apples."

George looked out at the apples on the ground motioning with his hand, "There's a heck of a lot of them this year. I'm separating the good ones from the ones with worm holes."

Frank jokingly replied, "People that get something for nothin', shouldn't aught to complain about getting a little fresh meat when they eat em!"

George laughed. "That's for sure. What can I do for ya? Who's that fella with ya?"

"This is my new neighbor. Ray just bought mum and dad's old place. He's from Philadelphia."

George smiled saying, "Tired of that city life are ya?"

"Yes: but I have to make a living somewhere and when I'm done, I intend to do just what you're doing right now, sit on my back porch watching the world go by."

He laughed as he stretched out his weathered hand to shake mine.

"Glad to meet ya." he said before sitting back down.

I couldn't help but notice his firm hand shake. They still had a lot of strength for a man in his advanced years. Unmistakably, they were the hands of a man who worked hard farming, and although the barn looked like it hadn't been used in quite awhile, he was still in great physical shape.

The tractor in the yard was covered with a heavy canvas, and grass was growing up around it.

The bottom of the sliding doors of the barn had grass growing up around it too, and there was no indication that dairy cows had taken refuge in the barn for many years. Testimony to that, the ground was undisturbed.

George was about 5' 5" -a thin man, and with his belt about six inches too long from losing weight, the excess hung down like a tongue. His yellow jacket was in need of a washing, but being older, he gave less concern for his appearance sitting on his own back porch, not expecting visitors.

The porch looked like something out of a Little Abbner cartoon comic strip. The chair he was sitting on was a faded maroon living room chair, with a gray throw rug on it as a cover. It obviously outlived its usefulness in the house, but was still good enough for the back porch.

A faded metal yellow cabinet was against the wall, and with the doors partially open, I could see a few old pots and some rusted coffee cans with nails and screws in them. A galvanized round wash tub hung on the wall by its handle suspended by a large nail, and a washboard that obviously saw many years of use, was leaning against the wall just below it. A small stack of wood was against the other wall with cinder blocks on either side holding the pieces in place, and a pile of outdated newspapers stacked next to them were held in place from being blown away by a brick.

Standing there, I got a whiff of smoke blowing down on the yard from the chimney, I assumed from a fire in a wood stove he used to heat the house. The screen door leading into the house was wood frame, and the full length screen had a bulge on the upper portion from being pushed open from inside.

The spring hinges that make the door close by itself, from age, had lost their strength and the door no longer closed tightly. Everything fit. It was a perfect picture for an older man living alone, the closing years of his life.

I said, "George, I hear you're the local water witch? I'd like to see how you do it someday, but right now I have a little bit of a problem at the house, Frank says you may be able to help me with."

"I'll be glad to try. What is it?"

Frank took over the conversation asking, "George, do you remember my sister having that problem with the ghosts in the house?"

"I'm not sure. It's been a long time; let me think for a minute. Is that when your mum sent her to town to live with your Aunt Ethel?"

"Yes, that's the time. Well, Ray here has the same problem and wanted to know if you'd be a fourth person in a séance tonight."

"I'll be glad to do it, but I don't know whether I have the gift. I tried it one time, but just couldn't get'er done. Funny though: for some reason my grandmother could sure talk in the spirit world. I'll giv'er a try. When you gonna do it?"

"Would it be ok if I picked you up around 6:00 o'clock?"

"That soon huh: I'll have to have my supper early then." Leaning over he picked up another apple to examine it then looked up, "I'll be right here waitin' on ya!"

On the ride back home I asked, "Frank, do you think at George's age it'll be a problem?"

"I don't think so. If it was, he would have told you no. Who's the person doing the séance?"

"It's someone I know from the city. She's a proven psychic."

"What do you mean by that?"

"She was able to locate bodies a few times for several police departments with some accuracy, and some of her predictions were downright uncanny."

He rolled back the bill of his cap as he did before, and I thought he was going to ask another question. When he didn't, and appeared to be just re-adjusting it on his head, I almost felt slighted.

I dropped him off at his driveway where I picked him up earlier and thanked him for introducing me to George. Looking at my watch I hadn't realized the time went by so quickly, it was almost 4 PM. I Thought, 'I hope Don and Delores don't think I abandoned them.' When I got to the house, they were in the kitchen.

When Don saw me he said, "We'll be more than happy to buy dinner."

I got the message loud and clear that they were hungry. After getting in the car, we headed for town. On the drive Delores inquisitively asked, "Will your neighbor be able to help?"

"He couldn't, but he took me to a guy that can. That's what took so long."

"Who is it, a different neighbor?" she asked.

"No, not exactly, he's the local water witch."

"A what:" Don skeptically exclaimed.

"You heard me. He's a water witch- what they call a dowser."

Don asked, "Will he be able to come tonight? I have to see this guy."

"He said he would. I told him I'd pick him up at his farm around six."

"Does he live far? It's almost 4:30 now." Delores asked.

"No, not very far from my place, I think you'll get a real kick out of George. He's 90 or more, and about as down to earth as you can get."

"You did say 90 plus? Isn't that a little old for him to take part in this?" Don asked.

"I guess we'll find out. Frank doesn't seem to think it's a problem. He said if George thought it would be, he wouldn't have volunteered."

We got to town only to discover the Chatterbox was closed.

"There's another restaurant just outside of town. Let's try there."

As we pulled into the parking lot, I said, "There aren't many cars on the lot, but it looks like it's still open. I haven't eaten here. I hope the food's good."

Opening the door we stepped in. The owner was turning stools upside down on the counter preparing to mop the floor and looked up acknowledging our entry.

I asked, "We're not too late are we?"

Looking up at the clock she replied, "Not yet: In another 20 minutes you would have been."

Here, as in the Chatterbox, Delores was once again amused at the prices asking, "I wonder if they would miss one of these menus. I'd like to take one back to Philadelphia to show the people at work."

Don leaned towards her quietly replying, "I hope they didn't hear you. No, let's not start Ray off on a bad foot. Leave the menu here!"

While we were eating, I noticed the sun beginning to set.

"I think we better hurry up. It's almost 5:30. I don't want to be late picking up George. How much do you have to do to get ready for the séance Delores?"

"Not much. How far does George live from here?"

"About 5 miles," I replied.

Hurriedly finishing dinner, we left for George's.

Chapter 9

When we arrived, he was sitting on the back porch with the light on waiting just as he promised. I walked him down to the car and held the door for him to get in.

"George, this is Delores and her husband Don. They're good friends of mine."

"Pleased to meet ya," he said shaking hands with them. He was holding an old square blue hand blown glass bottle. The glass was convoluted, which added a mystical look to its appearance and appeared to be quite old.

"George, what's that for?" I asked.

"It belonged to my great-grandmother, she had the power. Maybe it'll come in handy."

Delores asked, "What's the power and how did she use it?"

He began to explain with his frail voice, "My grandmother would put it in the middle of the table. When she went into a trance, someone would ask her a question and the bottle would spin and point to either YES or NO they had written on small pieces of paper at each end of the table."

"Did it ever work for you?" she asked.

"I tried-er once, but they wouldn't talk to me. I guess if I have questions to ask the spirits, I'll have to wait till I die and ask what I want in person."

We laughed.

Delores asked, "If you don't mind George, I'd like to try it. Maybe we can get a few answers of why the spirits aren't at rest."

I asked, "George, you said earlier you know about Frank's sister having the problem when she was young. What was that about?"

He replied, "I don't know the whole story. All I know is she had to go live with her Aunt Ethel from the beginning of October till after the first week in November. Ethel told me that one time, we're distant relatives. My grandmother was Frank's grandfather's sister."

I suddenly thought, "Maybe that's the connection. His grandmother is a sister to Frank's grandfather. That would make his sister at least have some psychic connection, she just didn't realize it. But why does it involve me?

"George, I met a neighbor last weekend at the Chatterbox. He told me about 10 years ago he saw the same apparition I saw the first night I arrived."

"Who was the neighbor?" he asked.

"His name was Dave. Do you know him?"

"Sure, he has the farm down the road from your place. What did he see?"

"He said a man driving a buggy passed him on the road as he was coming from his barn. The driver looked Amish and gave him an angry look, just like the one that passed me- just like the one I saw. He told me there was a woman sitting beside him staring straight ahead as it passed. He said, 'Within a few minutes after it went by, like I experienced, it disappeared. It was too short a time for it to have traveled out of sight. What could that mean?"

"I don't know. It could mean the same spirits are wandering the road trying to find whatever they're looking for. Did you ask what time of year it was?"

"Yes: he said it was about this time of year. If Frank's sister was having her problems during the month of October, we're within the same time frame and just might be successful finding out why they aren't at rest. Come to think about it, you mentioning wandering the road looking for something. The man that came to my door the first night I got here;

said he was looking for someone. He said the area looked the same, but the house and barn are different. He too, mentioned traveling up and down the road for a long time. I hope we can get this thing settled."

I looked over at Don, who seemed to be in deep thought about our weird conversation.

On the way back to the farm, we passed houses that George would give a little history lesson about. As we passed one, he said it was once a one room school house he attended when he was 9 or 10. You could see it was a school from the outline of the building but had several additions over the years, masking its original purpose. I thought it was interesting, but was more interested in my problem at hand, but I think Don welcomed his conversation. It broke his chain of thought worrying about the ghosts we may just meet in a short while. Pulling up in front of the barn, we walked up the hill to the front porch.

"George, that's where I saw the carriage coming from last week, when I arrived."

He didn't answer but gave me a bewildering look, and I discovered right there his hearing wasn't very good. Turning up the volume in my voice, I repeated it, this time looking at his face.

"George: last week when I got here, the carriage was coming from that direction. After I got to the porch and turned around, it was gone."

I still don't think he quite understood what I said even raising my voice, but he nodded then replied. "Maybe he was in a hurry."

Delores and Don smiled at his answer, and I decided to give up trying to explain anything else. Unlocking the front door, we went directly to the kitchen to set up for the séance. I didn't have much furniture, only a couch in the living room where I slept in my sleeping bag, an oil lamp, end table and the kitchen set with four chairs.

George asked, "Delores, why did you pick the kitchen to set up?" placing his finger to his chin as though he was about to hear a technical response. She was searching through her bag for a few candles when she looked up as if what he asked just registered in her mind.

"Oh, I'm sorry George, what did you say?"

"I asked why you're setting up the candles in here?"

Looking up from her search replied. "This is where I felt the most sensation, between the basement door and the stairs leading to the second floor where the sewing room is."

Continuing to search her bag, she had most of the contents on the counter before she said, "Ah, there they are. I thought for a minute I left them home."

Taking the six candles from the bag, she carefully placed them around the room. After lighting the first one, she began to light the second when a light breeze seemed to come out of nowhere putting out the flame. We looked at each other surprised, and I know everyone was thinking the same thing. We hadn't yet started, and there's already a presence. Did it go out on its own? Were we about to enter a world of spirits that were hostile? I thought to myself, 'We'll find out shortly.'

Lighting another match she cupped the flame with her hand, sheltering it from another unsuspecting breeze. After successfully lighting the others, she placed the blue bottle on its side in the middle of the table. George took two small pieces of paper from his pocket with *YES* and *NO* in capital letters written on them, and placed them at each end of the table. You could tell the letters were written by George, the letters were printed with jagged lines, a sign of an older unsteady hand. Delores instructed us to seat ourselves around the table in the order she asked. Her at one end, George at the other, with Don and I, on opposite sides of the table.

Delores asked, "Ray, would you turn off the light?"

I did as she asked then sat down. At her request, we held hands forming an unbroken circle. She began by closing her eyes seemingly concentrating, letting herself go into a trance. Our eyes were focused on what she was doing, and when she appeared to be fully in her trance, I asked the first question.

"Are you a Quaker?"

To Don and my surprise the bottle shook slightly then spun, stopping, pointing to the word *YES*.

Don and I looked at each other in amazement. The reaction of the bottle answering the question was uncanny. I could tell by looking at Don's face that he wasn't sure he wanted to continue being in the presence of a spirit we couldn't see. I didn't fear any immediate personal harm, but being truthful, a profound insecurity and a sense of fear crossed my mind.

I asked reluctantly, "Was there some sort of tragedy that happened to the family?"

The bottle again shook for a few seconds then spun around pointing to the word YES. At that point I looked at George's face. In the dimly candle-lit room, we could see his eyes were closed and he began to look pale and speak in a different tone of voice other than his own, a deeper__ younger man's voice.

It was obvious to Don and I that someone had invaded George's body, and we realized we didn't only have one spirit but two. Startling us even further, George jumped to his feet, tilted his head back with his eyes exposing only the white and yelled, "Adda! Get our son Joshua, and get out of the house. It's on fire!" repeating it several times.

Delores, in what seemed to be a panic stricken voice also foreign from her own, franticly yelled, "Levi, I can't find him! I can't find him! I'm trapped upstairs. Where are you?"

With fearful eyes quickly scanning the room, I noticed Don's face. It was probably like my own, frightened and shocked at what was taking place not knowing what to expect next.

The two restless spirits seemed to be re-enacting a tragedy that led to the haunting. Is this my problem? If it is: then why the hostility towards me? I had nothing to do with their event. The whole table began shaking at this point, and George seemed to go limp, falling back to his seat.

Fearing for his safety at his age, I didn't want the séance to continue, and I let go of his hand. Don did likewise, and after a few minutes, they both came out of their trance. After quickly turning on the light, I extinguished the candles.

Shaking their heads as if they were just waking from a deep sleep, they seemed to be trying to get their bearing. After a few minutes they appeared to be returning to normal, gathering their thoughts to where they are, verses where they had been. Don and I were waiting for Delores to speak; but were surprised when George spoke first.

"I think I bruised my knee," he said.

"George, you surprised us. You went into a trance too. You stood up from your chair and yelled, 'Adda, get our son Joshua and get out of the house. It's on fire!' You were speaking in a much younger voice. Do you remember anything?"

"I remember sitting there watching Delores in her trance, then I had a strange feeling come over me where I couldn't speak."

"What kind of feeling?"

"I felt like someone or something was taking over my body. They was tryin' to help somebody in trouble. Kind of, you know, desperate-like."

"You don't remember it?" I asked."

"No, all I know is I hurt me knee."

Don replied, "Maybe you hit it on the bottom of the table when you suddenly jumped up. The whole table was shaking. We wouldn't have noticed. Delores, what do you remember?"

"I felt I was in a state of panic, and the room was getting very warm. I could hear Levi's voice and was crying, looking for my son that's very young, possibly a toddler. I think I found him hiding under a bolt of cloth in the sewing room. He was crying, calling for his mommy and I remember picking him up," solemnly continuing, "But he was already dead."

When she mentioned the bolts of cloth, I remember the split second after opening the door to the sewing room, there was a toddler's leg sticking out from behind bolts of cloth.

I said, "Well, one thing's for sure, that would explain why you were feeling the room was getting hot. There must have been a fire."

As I listened to Delores and George, I knew there was a tragedy but couldn't figure out why they were in a house that was different from the original. According to the stone in the basement, when the original foundation was laid it had to be a one-story house.

George, still rubbing his knee, replied, "I can remember around 1910 or so, there was a fire here and a little boy as I recollect, died in that fire upstairs."

Delores commented, "Maybe the spirits were somehow swept into the more recent fire and it's very possible the boy died in the sewing room. Strange, at first I really felt content. I realized Adda's great love for her family. I actually experienced Adda getting vegetables to cook for dinner stored in the basement- then suddenly everything changed. I became panic-stricken. That's when I felt the intense heat."

Looking at George still rubbing his knee I asked, "George, how's the knee feel? Roll up your pant leg. I'll take a look."

He rolled it up, but there wasn't a mark I could see, he seemed fine. Getting up from the table he handed the blue bottle to Delores.

"Here, it's yours now. You keep it for your séances. You have the power to contact the spirit world. I don't have it. I'm satisfied just being a dowser."

Shaking my head, I thought, "Water witch, dowser, séances, ghosts and a bottle with mystical powers. If someone had told me these things were real a month ago, I would have thought they were crazy or drunk."

"It's getting late George. I better get you home."

Pulling up to his farm, I walked with him up the stone path until he was safely on the porch. With the porch light on, I could see a small branch in the shape of a Y. It was about 18 inches long, with 4 inches extending from where the two sides came together.

What appeared to be an old spring was lying next to it about 12 inches long, with a bolt stuck in either end. It was the type of spring tightly woven that was used years ago for pulling an old wooden screen door closed, similar to the one he has on his back door. When I picked it up to examine it, the end that was weighted by the bolt sagged down.

"George, what's the branch and the spring for?"

"That's what I use when I witch for water and other things. I thought I'd bring them just in case we needed them tonight, but I forgot."

"Maybe you'll have time to show me one of these days? I'm sure Delores would like to see how you do it too."

"Well, if you're not doing nothin' in the mornin', why don't you stop by? I always like to show a disbeliever how it's done."

"George, I wouldn't want to put a strain on you, but would you be interested in a second séance tomorrow evening?"

"I'll be glad to help. What time?"

"We'll make it earlier than tonight while it's still light. Let's say around 5 o'clock, if that's alright with you?"

"Why don't you make it around 1:00 o'clock? This way, I'll have time to show you how to witch water. Afterward, you can go to dinner, and I'll have my supper a little earlier than usual."

"You can have supper with us, if you'd like." I replied.

"No, that's alright. I'm an old man set in my ways. I'll be waitin' on the back porch."

I waited until he got inside, and he watched me through the window until I got in the car before turning out the porch light.

I went back to the farm for Delores and Don then headed back to the motel.

On the way, we decided to stop at a tavern we passed for a drink. I don't think any of us were tired, and we certainly weren't finished discussing the surprising events of the evening.

The place was smoke-filled and crowded with locals. Some were still in work coveralls, while others were in hunting camouflage pants and red hunting shirts. Bow hunting season began in earnest the beginning of October, and is a big sporting event here. The country music coming from the juke-box was barely audible over the different conversations, and we found a table the farthest from the bar. The waitress was Ruthie, the same person who waitresses at the Chatterbox, working a second job. Recognizing us she immediately said,

"Hello again: How are you finding what country livin's like?"

Don remarked, "Pretty interesting, but I don't know whether I could take a steady diet of it."

With demonstrating some home-spun philosophy, she replied, "Well, when you're born into it, it's different. We probably wouldn't care for the city life either," changing the subject she looked at me and continued, "How's the work on the house coming along?"

I replied, "Fine:" raising my eyebrows in a way that let her know I was only kidding.

She remarked, "Well things take time. I'm sure you'll get-er done eventually. Let me get your order into the kitchen."

After leaving Delores remarked, "She sounds like a philosopher."

"Yes she does." I replied.

After she brought back our order of beer and potato skins, Delores commented to me, "I can see your point. The life in a small town doesn't seem that bad. It didn't take very long for you to get acquainted with people."

"That's because they're outgoing. That's life in a small town. Oh, by the way, we have a lesson on how to witch water tomorrow afternoon. George is going to show us how it's done."

Surprised she asked, "How did this come about?"

"When I walked him to his back door, there was an old spring and a small tree branch on his chair. He said he forgot to bring them tonight."

Don asked, "What was he going to do with them?"

"I don't know. Maybe we can ask that question tomorrow."

We began a serious conversation about the séance, as we tried to sort out what had taken place. Delores, looking down at the ash tray, began spinning it on the table saying, "I felt an almost hysterical and angry sensation while I was in the trance too.

I was experiencing a vengeful feeling toward a man. I think his name may be Daniel." It was something Delores never mentioned to George.

I remarked, "The way you're spinning that ashtray- are you supposed to be mimicking the blue bottle?"

Appearing to be deep in thought about her experience, she suddenly broke a half-smile looking down at the ashtray as though she suddenly became conscious of her action replying, "No, not really. I'm still trying to figure it out," sarcastically continuing. "Besides, this ashtray is green glass, not blue."

I asked, "What do you think this all means? With you feeling anger, maybe it wasn't an accident and this person Daniel was somehow responsible for the fire that took the life of Adda and her son Joshua? Do you think there's a connection between the fire in the house and the Quakers in the carriage? If there is, we're dealing with four spirits, not two."

"Whoa! Ray. One thing at a time- The spirits in the coach so far are outside. We can deal with that later. There isn't enough information to tell. People that aren't in the trance are just as valuable a source of information as the person that is. In this case, I was drawn to Adda, maybe because I'm a woman and Levi to George, because he's a man that has some psychic ability too."

"That sounds plausible," I answered.

The increased noise in the bar was beginning to hinder our conversation, and we found ourselves having to almost shout across the table to hear each other.

The increased decibels were a combination of the patron's level of inebriation and some of the hunters arguing about the best technique to use when stalking white tailed deer. Others were encouraging the live four piece band that replaced the juke-box a half hour ago to play a certain favorite tune.

Almost having to shout to allow Don and Delores to hear me, I suggested, "Why don't we finish our drinks and leave?"

Don replied, "Sounds good to me. After what happened tonight, I'm ready for a little solace of my motel room."

We got up and inched our way through the overcrowded bar to the front door. When we got out to the parking lot, there was another crowd drinking beer sitting on the tail gates of some of the pickup trucks, engaged in similar conversations as the patrons inside. Several women in the crowd were wearing blue jeans and leather jackets with patches that matched some of the male bikers. The girls seemed to be a rough combination of feminism and masculinity in dress and manner, and Delores pointed out two of them as being quite attractive.

"Those two are probably the dominant factor in their relation-ships," she jokingly said.

We laughed and Don asked, "You're not thinking about buying a leather jacket and a whip, are you Delores?"

"No, just mentioning it."

After getting in the car, we drove to the motel and settled into our different rooms.

Still wide awake, I sat on the edge of the bed wondering if we were going to find out anything new on Saturday evening. Finally laying it aside for awhile and after a warm shower, it was time for bed. It seemed like my head had just hit the pillow when I heard a knock at the door adjoining our rooms.

"Are you ready for breakfast? We're hungry," Don asked.

"Yes, I'll meet you downstairs as soon as I'm dressed."

When I got to the cafeteria, Don and Delores were almost finished breakfast. It was the standard continental fare with a few extras that came with the room. I got some waffles and a cup of coffee then joined them at the table. We talked about going out to the place early to see if we could find out anymore than we already knew.

Overnight the air turned chilly, and on the ride to the farm, Delores commented again on how the beginning of fall was her favorite time of year. Immediately after pulling up in front of the barn, Frank's pickup came up the road and stopped. June was in the truck with him and they both stepped out anxious to hear what, if anything- happened during the séance.

"Hi Frank: good morning. I want you to meet some friends of mine from the city. This is Don and his wife Delores. Delores, this is June and Frank, my neighbors."

After shaking hands Frank said, "Glad to meet ya." then quickly asked, "Is she the psychic you told me about?"

"Yes, I guess you're wondering what happened last night?"

June quickly replied, "Yes, we sure are. We've been talking about it all morning, waiting to see when you'd show up."

"Well, quite a bit happened. We were able to contact two spirits and found out there was a fire in the house that possibly killed a toddler."

Looking surprised June asked, "Who got possessed? Was it you Delores?"

"Yes: I was possessed by a woman named Adda."

I interrupted, "We were surprised. George became possessed by a man named Levi."

They looked at each other in astonishment of what they were hearing. It didn't sound like a lie. Could it be some grand scheme to bring attention to the old house__ if it was, for what purpose?

Frank paused for a moment, raising the bill of his cap. "I remember my sister waking up one night and sleep walked downstairs. She woke everybody up in the house screaming, 'The house is on fire! They're two men dressed in black fightin' in the living room. One hit the other one on the leg with a hatchet.' Then she screamed again. I remember everyone running downstairs thinking the house was on fire. It scared the hell out of all of us. I remember my father shaking her until she woke up. As I remember, that seemed to be the first time it happened. She kept getting worse and worse. That's why dad shipped her off to Aunt Ethel's."

After Frank told us about the men fighting and one being hit on the leg, Delores and I both looked at each other with the same thought in mind, simultaneously remarking,

"Maybe that's the reason George felt the pain on his knee. If that's the case, he was being possessed by Levi, and there must be a third spirit in the house. That may be the spirit that caused the water in the shower to suddenly turn super hot. If it is, he's the one that's potentially dangerous."

Frank asked, "What do you mean turned the water hot?"

"Yes, Frank. When I was taking a shower, the water suddenly turned scalding hot."

Delores said, "Ray, if you and Don could ask some questions at the séance tonight, we might be able to find out more."

Frank and June seemed to be hanging on every word, intensely interested in our strange conversation. "If you're having another séance tonight, would you mind if Frank and I join you?"

"I don't mind, if Delores doesn't think it'll be a problem. You'll have to bring two chairs though. I only have four chairs with my kitchen set. Frank, I have to pick up George at 5. Want to come along?"

"I'd like to."

"Ok, I'll pick you up at 4:30."

They seemed excited we invited them and watched as they walked back to their pickup truck in conversation, then start back down the hill. I was reassured that Frank and his wife would be great neighbors.

During the morning, Delores swept out the upstairs, while Don helped me carry out the old carpeting and linoleum I had piled in the dining room from the previous weekend. While Don and I were working, Delores used my car to get to town and buy more cleaning supplies, and while she was there, picked up lunch. When she returned she remarked,

"You must have been working hard. The both of you are pretty dirty."

"Yes, I couldn't begin to tell you how old those carpets are, or how long they've been on the floor."

We washed up the best we could, then Don jokingly remarked, "I'm not used to doing this kind of dirty work. I'll sure enjoy that shower and a clean set of clothes tonight."

Hurriedly, we had lunch then headed for George's. As we pulled into the driveway, he got out of his chair with the branch and old spring in his hand, tools of his trade.

"Ray, is that the branch and spring in his hand?" Delores asked.

"Yes, strange isn't it?"

"Good afternoon, are you ready for the demonstration?" George inquired.

Delores replied, "George, I've been ready since Ray told me about it last night."

Handing me the spring, George began the lesson.

"Here's how you hold the branch." Taking it with the end of each fork of the Y in his hands, he held it waist high with his elbows at his side and the branch straight out.

The four inches of branch that extended from where the two sides were joined were what I thought might be the part that extends to the ground.

Delores asked, "George, what kind of tree did you cut the Y fork from?"

"I cut my forks from a cherry tree, but they say any pitted fruit tree would do. Some folks only use the branch of a willow. They say a willow tree always seeks water because they grow so fast, and that's true. They always grow quicker near a stream or a wet area. Here, Delores, you hold it."

At her first attempt, she didn't hold it properly, and with a smile, George corrected her.

"Ok, now what do I do?" she asked.

Motioning with his finger, he said, "Walk slow right down through the yard there. If you have the ability to witch, the branch will point down to the ground where there's water flowing."

As she started down through the yard, George told her, "You're not running a foot race, walk slower."

As she passed a spot, the branch began pointing down. Stopping, she asked.

"George, I'm trying to hold the branch straight out as you told me, but it's hard to do. Am I doing something wrong?"

"Well, go forward and see if it comes back up."

After walking a few feet farther, the branch returned to its original position.

Don asked, "Are you doing that Delores?" laughing at her success.

"No, whatever it is, it's controlling the branch."

"Here Don, you try it." George said.

"No thanks. Let Ray do it."

I took the branch from Delores and following George's instructions, began walking slowly down through his yard.

"Look, George, the branch is pulling down right here. It's pulling hard too."

"Well, walk a little farther and we'll see what you do."

I walked farther, and the branch returned to its original position. A few steps farther and the branch pulled down again. Experimenting, I backed up and to my astonishment, the branch slowly returned to its normal position.

I walked slowly backward the rest of the way to the porch, and in every spot Delores and I walked over feeling a reaction, I got the same result. "Damn, this thing really works. It's uncanny," looking at George I remarked.

George laughed. "You sure you don't want to try it Don?"

"Ok, give me the branch," he replied.

Holding it the same way as Delores and I, he began walking down through the yard. No reaction, nothing. He might just as well be carrying a walking cane or an umbrella.

"I didn't feel anything, why not?" he asked.

"Well, not everybody does," George replied, "It's like the spirit world- certain people have the power but most don't."

I asked, "George, I know this is your yard, so I assume you've witched it before. Were we right where the branch pulled down?"

Turning around pointing, he said, "Do you see that small shed? That's the old spring house. Now look over at that cement slab. That's the well I use now. They're both in line with where you witched. Yes, you two graduated. How does it feel to be a water witch?"

Delores replied gleefully, giving George a hug. "It feels like you've added another page to my accomplishments. What's the spring for?"

"When I find a spot, I hold the spring by one end- fist clenched, with the bolt under my thumb, like this." Demonstrating as he did with the branch he held it out and said, "Here Ray, you try it."

Holding it as he instructed, I said, "George, the other end droops down."

"That's what it's supposed to do. Now stand over the spot where you felt the branch pull down the strongest."

Doing as he asked, in disbelief, the loose end started to bob up and down.

"What's happening? George, am I doing something wrong?"

"No, count how many times the spring bobs. For every bob, that's about a foot, telling you how deep you'll have to drill for the water."

Don quickly remarked, "You're kidding, right?"

"No sir: If you continue to hold it, it'll stop; then in a few seconds it'll start bobbing again. It will be half the count as the first time and the third time it starts it will be half of that count."

Holding it again, I tested his theory. Sure enough, his analysis of what would happen did exactly what he predicted.

"George, can I take the branch and spring home and try it in my yard?"

"Sure, you can give them back when you're finished with them."

After an hour of conversation about George's accomplishments, we left and returned to the farm. Another hour of cleaning and we were ready to go for dinner. It was getting late in the afternoon and I wondered where the day had disappeared to so quickly. I had to pick up Frank at 4:30 then drive out to get George.

After picking him up, I told him about the lessons in witching George gave us. He seemed more interested in talking about the séance, and talked about it all the way to George's asking questions I didn't have an answer to. When we got to his house, he was waiting on the back porch just as he promised. Getting out of his chair with an unsteady hand, he grasped the porch post to keep his balance. I quickly got out of the car and hurried up the path to help him.

"Are you sure you want to come tonight? You look a little unsteady. Is it because of the knee?"

"No: just an old man's failings. When I got home last night, the knee didn't hurt anymore and when I looked this morning, there still wasn't any bruise.

Hurt like hell at the time though. Hello, Frank, I see they got you involved too."

"No, it wasn't my idea, it was June's. I don't know whether I'm going to like this or not. I hear you were giving lessons today on witching, did they pass or fail?"

"They both passed, Don failed. He couldn't do it."

I helped George to the car, and he seemed shaky. Skeptical about his involvement I asked again, "You sure you want to go George? I don't want anything to happen to you."

"No, I'll be fine."

When we got to the farm, as I figured, Delores and Don had already filled June in on what took place last night. The table was ready to go with the *YES* and *NO* papers at each end, and the blue bottle was on its side in the middle. The candles were also in place where they were the night before, and walking into the kitchen, I lighted each one then turned out the light.

I couldn't help but notice the way June and Frank were wide-eyed, apprehensively gazing around the candle lit room. Although we were seated, the flames flickering from the candles made our shadows on the walls seem as if they were moving. Frank, warily looking around, seemed astonished that a room so familiar to him, the very room he and his family had numerous meals in, harbored such a history. I could only imagine it was beyond the scope of his imagination, and he looked as though he wasn't anxious to discover the secrets he never knew.

Chapter 10

We finally settled in the order Delores directed. Her at the head, George at the far end, with Frank and June on one side, Don connected to Delores and me on the opposite side. She began by asking us to join hands. Closing her eyes and slowly bowing her head in an almost reverent manner, she seemed to be going into a trance, a world she was familiar with. In a monotone voice she asked, "Adda, are you with us tonight?"

After a few moments, her hair fluffed up. Slowly raising her head she opened her eyes staring at the blue bottle, a stare that was completely blank and seemed to be devoid of our presence. Her lips began to quiver and she began to speak in a different tone of voice, alien once again from her own.

"Yes, I'm here. Where's Levi?"

All our attention had been on Delores, when suddenly we looked at George. Without noticing, he had already been possessed apparently by Levi. Staring at the blue bottle, he quickly answered, "Adda, I'm here. I know you're here, but you seem to be in a different house, not our own. The rooms are different. Where are you?"

I thought to myself, "George was right. The bottle does have mystical powers."

Quick thinking on June's part, she asked the same question Delores asked before she went into her trance.

"Adda, are you here with us?"

Frank was surprised June was so eagerly involved, glancing at me as though I somehow had an answer to his inquiring look. He seemed to want reassurance from me that no harm would come to him if he didn't immediately flee the house, escaping the spectacle he was witnessing. We were familiar with the change in George's voice, but Frank and June were startled, knowing it wasn't his normal tone. They weren't here last night to witness it. It was a deeper, youthful voice completely foreign to their ears. It wasn't George speaking, it was Levi. The spirits that were manifested began a conversation, as if they were only using the physical means of communicating through Delores and George, as if we weren't in the room.

"Adda, has Daniel been here today?" Levi said through George.

"Yes, he makes me uncomfortable when I'm here alone with him," Adda replied through Delores.

"There's no need to fear Daniel. We've been friends for a long time, since we were children."

June quickly asked, "Are you and Levi husband and wife?"

The bottle spun gently in a slow motion as if it was content to answer, stopping, it pointed to the word *YES*. We realized we were witnessing a conversation between a husband and wife that happened over 200 years ago. There was a moment of silence before I asked, "Levi, were you the one fighting with a person in the living room?"

The bottle shook violently then spun a complete revolution pointing to the word *YES*- the paper on the table in front of June.

June drew back her head, frightfully looking down at the bottle as if it would cause her some harm. The look on her and Frank's face was as if they had actually seen a ghost. I could see they were both wide-eyed, and it looked as though they wanted no part with continuing, instead, wanted to exit the house quickly as possible. Realizing it, I presented my next question to Adda, hoping it would attract June's attention making her less frightened listening to Adda's gentle voice.

I asked, "Why do you feel uncomfortable with Daniel?"

With a brief moment not knowing if she would answer, Adda finally broke the temporary silence of the room.

"His sister Salema warned me that he was still containing a rage because I rejected his offer of marriage, but Levi dismisses that because they had been friends since childhood."

Don surprised me when he asked, "Was the fire in the house accidental?"

The bottle rattled on the table as if something was holding it back from giving the answer, but after a few seconds of struggling back and forth, it finally turned to the word *NO*. Don quickly asked Adda another question. "Did Daniel start the fire?"

The bottle shook violently this time turning in the direction of the word *NO*.

Suddenly, it seemed to be overpowered and dramatically reversed, rattling and shaking the whole table until it settled pointing to the word *YES*. It appeared there was another spirit present, who was obviously angered at the question, preventing the bottle from giving the correct answer. George startled us when he suddenly stood up staring at the ceiling; then yelled out loud, "Adda, quick! Get Joshua and get out of the house. It's on fire!"

With my clasped hand holding Franks, I could feel his palm sweating. He began pulling away from mine and I grasped it a little tighter, preventing his release so it wouldn't break the human chain. There was too much at stake, and I didn't want the séance to end until we found out more. Don and I realized it was Daniel in his anger that set the fire and maybe after setting it, Levi walked in catching him in the act. I quickly asked Adda, "Did Daniel know you were in the house when he started the fire?" Again, the bottle turned slowly to the word *NO*, as if Daniel didn't want to interfere with Adda's answer.

George yelled, "What are you doing Daniel? Adda's in the house with our son Joshua."

At that point, George groaned and grabbed his knee. When he did, the chain was broken, but the possessions didn't stop. They grew stronger, and all of us who were conscious wanted it to end. An air of anger swept through the room so strong everyone sensed it. A kitchen cabinet door opened and we turned to look, hoping it was a loose hinge, until it slowly closed again on its own. Another door opened a little quicker then slammed shut.

Our eyes were following the activity in the room with astonishment, sending our heads in the direction of every new movement. A drawer suddenly opened, exposing its contents then closed by itself. Another drawer opened, then another. Cabinet doors began rapidly opening and closing on their own and fear suddenly swept over the room. To add to the crescendo of horror, the light that had been turned off began flickering on and off. With the cabinet doors opening and closing faster and more violent, one of the cabinet doors split down the middle, sending the severed end hurling across the room. Dishes and cups began falling from the shelves, smashing on the floor.

At this point everyone was frightfully looking at one another by all the spirit activity in the room, wondering what would happen next.

Surprisingly, Don became involved and asked, "Adda, why did you reject Daniel?"

Asking that question seemed to subdue the activity of the cabinets, as if Daniel was waiting for the answer from Adda that he had been lamenting for 200 years.

"He was too possessive and accusing, even when I would speak to my friends. My friend Sarah is married to Daniel's older brother. She stopped by my parent's one afternoon to seek temporary shelter from the rain. When she walked in, Daniel was in a rage, accusing my parents of causing our separation. She told me, as she was leaving the house, she asked him to come home with her, but instead he ran out into the storm. Pleading, she called to him again, but he wouldn't listen.

Sarah's parents tried to warn me and Levi several times of his feelings, and to be careful and not be too trusting. They knew their son was having a problem with my rejection and were worried, fearing for Levi's life and mine."

The candles were growing dim, and Delores came out of her trance. It seemed that the confrontation between spirits was at an end for the evening, and I think Frank and June were as glad as Don and I.

I asked, "George, do you remember what you were sensing when you groaned?"

"I felt anger, a feeling I never had before, it felt strange like." trying to recall exactly what he experienced he continued, "I think I might have been fightin' with a fella. He was swinging a hatchet at me when I was on the floor. I was trying to fight him off, but it wasn't doin' no good. He just kept at it. I thought he hit me on the knee. I felt a sharp pain on the side of my head, then after that I didn't feel nothin'."

"Do you remember anything else George?" I asked.

"I could hear a woman's voice. I think she was screaming my name, sort of in a state of panic. She kept yellin'. I think she was sayin', 'Levi, I'm upstairs. I can't find Joshua.' I kept hearin' it until the voice and the anger just seemed to fade away."

I quickly remarked, "Don, they say the last sense to go when you're dying is your sense of hearing. It's possible what George was feeling was the first hatchet blow to his knee and torso- then the fatal blow to the head."

Frank and June, both still trembling like all of us, got up from their chairs surveying the damage to the room and broken dishes on the floor. They were sweating like the rest of us, but they were also nervously relieved that the séance was over.

Stepping carefully through the debris, I closed the few drawers and cabinet doors that were open. I picked up the piece of cabinet door that was split in half and examined it. The force that was needed to do that kind of damage was powerful. On the edge where the wood was exposed, I noticed the door was made out of Maple, an extremely hard wood. Now I had my answer to the sudden increase in hot water- Daniel's spirit was violent.

"George, do you want me to take you home?"

"I think so. I'm a little tired."

"Ray, while you're taking him home, I'll get the broom and clean up this mess." Delores said.

June remarked, "I'll help."

I said, "Delores, after you finish, go with Frank and June. I'll join you after I get back,"

Don looked relieved that he didn't have to remain in the house until I returned, and testimony to that, he began helping clean up to get finished a little quicker.

"George, let me help you with your jacket. Thanks for coming."

"Call on me anytime," he replied.

"We're heading back to the city tomorrow, but I hope to come back next weekend, will you still be available?"

"If the good Lord's willing, and I'm still alive. I don't have anything planned. I'll be here."

"I pulled into George's driveway and walked with him up the path to his porch. He went inside and waited until I got back in the car before switching the porch light on and off, letting me know he was safely inside, then I drove back to Frank's.

When I arrived, everyone was sitting around the dining room table, drinking coffee and talking about what each other felt and observed. The excitement for the night was over, but Frank was more interested in the house he grew up in and had no idea there was such a tragic story behind its history. The experience confirmed to him the nightmare his sister had to endure in her young life, no one else in the family was aware of.

Frank said, "When those cabinet drawers and doors started opening and closing by themselves, my first instinct was to get the hell out of there just as fast as I could. The only thing stopping me was June squeezing the hell out of my one hand, and your tight grip Ray, on the other. I didn't want to look like a coward, especially in front of my wife. So I stayed."

"Delores, what do you think is the reason for the cabinet doors and drawers opening and closing so violently?" I asked.

"From what you're telling me of my reaction, and the conversation with Levi through George, it's obvious the spirit that's present is probably Daniel. He seems to be harboring anger to the house that gives refuge to the woman he still loves and the man she married."

"Then why doesn't he affect all of us, instead of just certain people?"

"That's a question I don't have an answer to, but the fact that he only affects certain people could mean they themselves have some psychic ability. More than likely; and I don't know for sure, since the anger could be coming from Adda or Levi, they may be desperately trying to get someone's attention to help them. I do feel somehow the carriage you experienced the night you arrived has something to do with the night of the fire, but I don't understand what. People that aren't in the trance are valuable. They can ask pertinent questions and are able to critique after the séance. With all my experiences, the people in a trance most of the time, don't remember what takes place. They're sort of in a suspended animation with someone else controlling their mind. Feelings are different; they're a state of mind of the spirit that actually enters my body. It's obvious that George is the same. With only feeling the pain in his knee tonight, it sounds like the spirit of Levi entering his body is becoming stronger. Tonight he was able to tell us more."

Frank remarked, "Maybe its Adda's parents in the carriage, coming to warn them about Daniel and what they feared he might do."

"I never thought of that Frank, but that would make sense," Delores replied.

June remarked, "Instead of being unprepared like we were tonight, we should write a few questions down we'd like to ask. I'll get a pencil and paper." Returning to the table, she asked, "Delores, what question should we ask first?"

"The first question we should ask is why Adda was home alone that night with her son. The second question should be what, if anything did the carriage, the Quaker couple and the barn have to do with that night?"

Excitedly, June asked, "Ray, are you coming up next weekend? If you are, I mean, if you're having another séance, we'd like to be here."

Frank, wide-eyed, quickly looked at June as if to say, "Thanks for volunteering me, but after tonight's episode, I would have liked the opportunity to be silent."

"Ray, I hope you're coming up." Delores said, "I want to get down to the real reason for this haunting. This by far, is a haunting with the most active spirits I've ever encountered."

"I'll be willing to come up. I'd like to get it resolved one way or another, before I begin the work on the place to make it livable without all these manifestations. I know it sounds like a line from a horror story, but I wouldn't want to be working on a project in the house and turn around to see Daniel standing behind me with a hatchet in his hand."

Don looked at me and replied, "Now that's dramatic."

After saying goodnight to June and Frank we left for the motel.

I wanted to get an early start in the morning and get back to the city to catch up on some unfinished work when I left the office on Thursday, not wanting to impose too much on Mr. Johnson's good will.

With the skyline of the city coming into view, it didn't take long to get to Don and Delores's. After dropping them off, I returned to my apartment, and immediately got into my work.

Chapter 11

I stayed at work an extra two hours each day as I did last week not wanting to fall behind. On Wednesday, I was about to pick up the phone to call Don when it rang. Talk about being psychic. Before I could say hello, Delores excitedly asked. "What time are we leaving on Friday?"

Knowing her interest would be compounded by what we experienced, I jokingly replied, "I didn't think you wanted to go, so I made other plans."

Quickly responding, "You creep: I've been talking about what happened all week. We want to get to the farm early."

I laughed then responded, "Delores, before any more insults calling me a creep, I took off Friday again. I can pick you up in the morning at 8:00 if it's all right with you."

"All right with us: Make it in the morning as early as you can."

"Ok, ok, I'll be there."

"That's great, we'll be waiting. Oh: by the way. I hope you don't mind, I spoke to a friend about what happened, she's also a psychic. She wanted me to ask if she could come with us. Her name is Susan."

"Is she as good as you?"

Ignoring my question she excitedly rattled on, "I spoke to her this week, she had some interesting things to say, and yes, she's not only as good as me- she's better. She's also attractive and divorced without any current attachments."

In a less interested voice I commented, "I'd wish you'd stop trying to match mate me. I'm happy for right now. That's not the real reason for her being invited, is it?"

"No: she's every bit of a professional. When I told her about George and the mysterious blue glass bottle, she almost begged me to go."

"Since you say that her credentials are better than yours- something I can hardly believe, I don't mind. The more input the better."

"Ok, now that we got the B.S. out of the way, what time are you picking us up?"

"Like I said, I'll be there around 8:00, the same as last Friday."

On Friday, I drove to Don's. Pulling up in front of the house, Delores introduced her friend as soon as I got out of the car.

"Ray, this is Susan."

Extending my hand I said, "Pleasure to meet you Susan. Would you mind if I just called you Sue?"

"I don't mind at all. In fact, I'd prefer it."

She was every bit of what Delores described. Attractive, very attractive, and I might add, well built also. She was blond, about the same age as Delores, but a little taller, about five feet five inches.

"I hear you have boarders that aren't paying rent," she amusingly said.

"Yeah, but they're boarders I can do without. Delores tells me you're also a psychic, and better than her."

She replied, "I don't believe the better than her part, but yes, I'm also a psychic. And please, don't give me the strange look I always get when someone asks that question."

I replied, "Well, it's certainly a statement you don't hear every day, but I guess their looks are sometimes warranted."

"After your experiences the last couple of weekends, what do you think of the occult?" she asked.

"You didn't see me give you that look you just described; the look you claim most people give you when you tell them__ did you?"

"No, I guess you're safe."

It was the last weekend of October, and on the drive I noted how the trees were in full color in and around the city.

"Yes Ray," Sue remarked, "They're beautiful. The problem is; they won't last very long. The other day when I was walking to the store, I was stepping on the leaves listening to them crunch.

It reminded me of when I was a kid stepping on the biggest ones. What stage are the leaves in at the farm?"

"The peak is past but I think they're still enough on the trees that will make it look colorful."

The drive seemed quicker than normal probably because it was filled with conversation about the weekend before. Sue was actually the focal point on most of the trip, and it was interesting listening to some of her experiences in dealing with the spirit world. Some of her stories were almost parallel with our séance.

I hadn't known from Delores, but Susan talked about a psychic experience she had in Frankford. I realized Sue must have been the person Delores was telling me about, the one working with the apparitions of the Quakers in the Sullivan's home. If what Delores told me was true, she probably is just as good as her or as Delores described, 'Even better.'

As we neared our exit I was happy to see for Susan's sake, most of the leaves were still on the trees. Turning toward the farm she remarked, "This area is beautiful! The farms and valleys in fall color are like a painting."

I was happy she said so, and knew her opinion would soon change after she saw the inside of my house.

"Ray, let's get a late lunch at the Chatterbox," Delores suggested.

Sue asked, "Ray, what's the Chatterbox? Sounds like a day care center."

"I'll let Delores tell you. She's been there."

"Sue, it's the friendliest restaurant you'll ever eat in and the food's great." Being coy she added, "You have to watch out for the prices though, they're out of hand."

Delores and I looked at each other with a smile, knowing she was leading Sue on.

Sue replied, "If they're that bad, we can go somewhere else. I don't have to eat an expensive lunch."

Looking at each other we smiled again knowing she was unaware of what she was about to learn when we got there. I was happy when she said, 'We don't have to eat an expensive lunch.' That thought would have never entered my ex's mind.

As we reached the edge of town, Sue read aloud the brightly colored, hand-carved sign: "Welcome to Canton."

"Well, here it is!" I announced, "The fair Metropolis of Canton, population about 2,000."

Don quickly replied, "Where are they hiding? I haven't seen a 150 people on two trips here. They must be counting the same people more than once."

I laughed.

As we drove down Main Street, I pointed out the Rialto Theater, the Sentinel newspaper, the Library and Jim's Gun Shop.

Sue said, "Looks like a quaint little town to me. I'll bet living here isn't that bad."

I replied, "I'll know better after I move here in 20 years. I know one thing for sure. It's going to be less crowded and probably a lot less expensive than living in the city."

Turning in my direction Don replied, "Ray, I've known you for a long time. I would have never guessed a person like you would have made a move like this,"

"Why's that, Don?" Sue asked inquisitively.

"Well Sue, first of all, he loves the baseball games and football games we go to and he has a lot of friends. It seems to me he'll have to give up a lot of his current lifestyle. I guess my question is will he be happy doing that?"

"Wait a minute Don," I replied, "I have news for you. I was thinking about it for two years now, ever since Charles got married and left our group."

"Who's Charles?" Sue asked, seemingly more interested in our conversation.

"He's one of the guy's in the city we hung around with. He married a girl from Colorado that worked in Philadelphia at the time. She went back home to help her mother that became terminally ill with cancer. Her mother owned a 200 acre ranch, 50 miles outside of Denver. I still keep in touch with them. He told me it took awhile to get used to, but since then, he's become a regular cowboy. Not that I'm old or decrepit, but how long do you think I'm going to keep going to sports bars Don? Let's face it, the city's getting more expensive to live in every year and eventually you'll have to wake up to that reality."

"What reality:" he replied.

"Don, my father had a saying that still rings true today. 'You better be living where you can afford to be, 10 years after you retire.'

"That sounds like a man with a lot of common sense," Sue remarked.

"That doesn't even begin to talk about the intangibles," I continued, "The people aren't in a rush here, and I don't have to circle the block three times before I find a parking space. I'll give you an example. I went to the supermarket last week."

Don interrupted with a little sarcasm in his voice, "You mean the super market we passed when we got to town, the one that was a supermarket when it was built in the 1950s?"

"Yes, that's it. I was standing in the checkout line when the person in front of me started a conversation with the cashier. I was becoming very impatient waiting then suddenly realized there was no reason to rush. Luckily, I decided to wait for five more minutes before clearing my throat, reminding them I was still waiting. It was the same way at the bank where I opened up an account. Unlike the city where you have two tellers and 20 people waiting, I saw three tellers and two patrons. These are small examples we never notice living in the city."

"That's a funny story, Ray," Sue said before continuing, "Come to think about it, I had the opposite experience at the supermarket the other day. I only had to buy a quart of milk and there was a long line. I was late for an appointment and politely asked an elderly woman closer to being checked out if I could get in front of her.

She agreed, but a person behind her began taking issue with her letting me in."

"What happened then?" I asked.

"Well, rather than make a scene, I thanked the woman and started walking to the end of the line when a guy who was two people behind the old woman let me in front of him. He was big and burly, and I didn't hear anyone behind him objecting. Not even the guy that was giving the old woman grief."

"Sue, that's called common courtesy. It's in abundance here. It was also that way in Western Pennsylvania where my father moved after he retired."

"I would have liked to have met your father," she said, "He sounds like a real philosopher."

"If you ever had a conversation with his father, you'd realize how much of an understatement that is," Delores added.

Delores changed the subject. "If we get a chance and can use Ray's car this afternoon, I'd like to look in some of these small shops on Main Street. They're probably locally owned. Look! There's even an antique shop we could browse."

I interrupted their conversation. "Well, if you ladies don't mind, let's see if we can get my problem fixed first."

"Ok, Ray," Sue said. "We didn't forget your problem. Where is this Chatterbox?"

"It's on the other side of this intersection, and I might add, the only traffic signal in town."

After parking on the lot, we went inside.

Walking in Ruthie looked up from wiping a table and said, "Hi Ray, you people find a seat. Here are a few menus. I'll be with you in a minute."

Susan looked around and in almost a whisper asked, "Is this place where I'll be shocked at the prices on the menu?"

I replied, "Yes, but not the way you thought. Look at it."

The lunch crowd was thinning out, and we found a table for four next to the front window.

"This place from the outside looks like it may have been a store or showroom for something," Sue noted, "These windows are almost floor to ceiling."

"I thought the same thing the first time I was here. I examined the building from the outside. There's a weathered sign near the top that reads 'Packard Auto Sales and Garage.' This must have been the showroom. The restaurant is only a small part of the building. There's several other small businesses attached, and what looks like apartments on the floors above."

Taking in my description of the building, she opened the menu. Quickly closing it, she remarked as she stood up as if she was ready to leave then smiled. "I think these prices are outrageous! Let's get out of here."

We laughed, and I thought to myself, "She has a neat sense of humor. I wonder whether her humor would still be intact after she sees the house, and realizes her opinion of my common sense wasn't misguided."

Ruthie came to the table. "Ray, I see you brought an extra set of hands this weekend, are you ready to order?"

"Yes, I think we're ready."

Laughing, she replied, "Still remember my name, huh? That's really impressive. What's your pleasure today?" continuing with a smile. "We have a special on chili- cup or bowl same price!" Looked up at the clock she added, "We're going to close in an hour. Tomorrow it will be left-overs. What'll it be?"

Laughing at her salesmanship, she took our order and returned to the kitchen.

I noticed Sue taking it all in- the restaurant, the customers and the waitress. I could tell it was all foreign to her.

"Sue, living in a small town's different. Everyone seems to know everyone else's business."

"Yes, it sure seems that way. How did you ever find this place?"

"Well, it took two years of looking."

Then I related the story of how it happened telling her the circumstances. I looked at so many properties, but none of them suited me. I didn't care what shape the property was in. I just had a certain criteria in mind for a farm and adamantly stuck with it. The difficult part is, after looking for a period of time, I began to get frustrated and was almost willing to take anything.

The real estate agent was also getting at the end of his patience showing me properties, and after about six months, was tired of taking me around. He began making all sorts of excuses about being with other clients.

When I had the feeling he was putting me off, I went to his office and asked why he was giving me the brush off on the phone. He told me there were people that come up and just look. He felt he was wasting a lot of time on a person that wasn't serious about buying. When I told him I was a definite sale, he opened his desk drawer and gave me a file card of a farm that had been vacant for a long time, save one purchaser that never occupied it, and only owned it for two years.

I looked at him and asked the directions to the place. He looked back at me, examining the card identifying the house, barn and acreage. It seemed to be just what I was looking for, so I drove to the vicinity where he explained it was. After traversing a few roads I gave up on finding it. Thinking it may have been a gag property to humor me, I returned to his office and asked, "Is this supposed to be a gag? I drove up and down all the roads you described and couldn't find it."

"No, the property's there, let me get the key, I'll take you to it."

"He drove me out to see it, and while he was showing me the barn, I agreed to buy it and wrote a deposit check sealing the sale.

Don chimed in, "But the farm house itself is a 10 year project if not more. I have to confess though, with what Ray knows about construction, anything he bought could be redone to his liking."

"What made you settle on this place if it's as bad as Don says?" she asked.

"I wanted at least 50 acres or more with a certain amount of woods and cleared ground. I wanted a view, unlike my father's property in Western Pennsylvania- in a valley.

I really wanted a pond on the property but after two years of looking. I settled for a stream running through the property instead. It has everything else I wanted."

"The view is real nice," Don added. "It's the one thing that's a positive. It's up to Ray, but I think he should just tear it down and start over."

"Sue, I like the style of older homes. They have character. I don't like the ones that look like cracker boxes with a roof." Surprisingly, she agreed.

When Ruthie returned to the table with our food, she teased, "Can't stand being away from here, can ya?" as if she had known us for years. She remembered seeing Don and Delores the week before at the restaurant and the bar, but didn't recognize Sue.

"You're new to this group. What do you think of our little corner of the world, kinda different, ain't it?"

Sue laughed, "Yes, a lot different."

After lunch we went to the hardware store to pick up an added flashlight and more batteries then proceeded to the farm. When we pulled up to the barn, Sue asked, "Is this where you pulled up the first night you arrived?"

"No, I pulled up in front of the older section," pointing, "About 30 feet further."

"It's important to park in the same location. I'd like to go into the barn first before we go in the house."

I moved the car forward as she asked, and we got out. Sue walked into the barn just as Delores had the first day, with us following.

"I want to see if I feel a presence the same way Delores said she felt, going from the new section to the old."

"Just watch your step Sue. Some parts of the floor are soft."

"Ok, I'll be careful." She walked slow heeding my warning.

Following her from a comfortable distance, we anxiously watched for any reaction as she passed from the new to the old section. Would she feel more of a presence? We couldn't tell. All of a sudden she hesitated. Hesitated at the same spot Delores had on her encounter. All of us could feel a definite change in temperature and looked at each other then refocused on Susan.

She suddenly glanced up as if she was aware of something we couldn't feel, something Delores didn't even respond to. Strangely enough, it was exactly where the two barns were connected together.

After we got outside, I asked, "You seemed to be a little hesitant when you got to where the barns were connected. Did you sense something different?"

"I experienced a temperature difference, and a great sorrow of someone who lost a loved one, but that's not much help."

"Why isn't it much help?" I asked.

"They could be two completely different incidents."

"That's not very reassuring. I'm not living in the barn though. That's getting torn down. So the house is really my priority."

While we were standing next to the barn, Frank, who had seen us as we passed, came up to say hello. Getting out of his truck, he remarked, "Hi, Delores, are you ready for another scare- the- hell- out- of- me session this weekend?"

We laughed. "Are you and June coming tonight?" Realizing I hadn't introduced Sue I said, "Oh, I'm sorry Sue. This is Frank, my neighbor. He and his wife June were here last Saturday night. Frank, this is Sue a friend of Delores'. She's also a psychic."

"Pleased to meet ya'. My wife and I will be coming up tonight. She has something she wants to tell you. It happened right here by the barn

Tuesday night, just before a rain storm__ Scared the hell out of her and the dog too!"

"What happened?"

"I'll let her tell you. I don't want to spoil it. I guess you're going to start about 6:00?"

"No Frank, probably earlier, about 5:00."

"Good! We'll bring an extra chair for Susan."

"Thanks, that'll be great. I have to pick up George at 4:30. Care to go along?"

"I'd like to."

"I'll pick you up at four."

As we walked up the front lawn to the porch, Sue turned around and stood scanning the view.

"This view of the valley's panoramic, really neat. You can see several miles in every direction. I understand now what Don was saying about a beautiful view."

When I opened the front door she hesitated, then laughed. "Now I know what Don was saying about being a major project."

I was disappointed in her remark but wasn't shocked. She didn't have to elaborate, the place is a disaster. Going inside, I realized even with the chill in the air, the house seemed cooler than it should have been. The sun shining all day through the windows without shades or curtains should have made the place at least a little warmer.

Delores remarked as she closed the door, "It's chilly in here!"

"I'll turn up the thermostat. I turn it down when I'm not here."

I went to the dining room to turn it up, but when I looked, I was surprised. I forgot to turn it down when I left last weekend. The house shouldn't have been cool at all. I tried the light switch thinking the power was off for some reason, but the light went on. I thought, 'The power's on, I wonder if there's a problem with the furnace? I hope not.' Turning up the thermostat to 80 degrees, I could hear the furnace kick on. That's a relief. I don't have to do anything immediately with changing the old bugger.

"Ray, is there something wrong with the heater?" Don asked.

"No, everything's under control. I was afraid there was, but it seems to be fine now, the house will be warm soon."

When Delores called Sue to tell her about the experience she had last weekend, she only told her the basics. If Susan agreed to come, Delores didn't want to have her mind contaminated with the experiences she felt.

She wanted to show Sue the house without us, and I was confident she knew enough about its history, to do so.

"Ray, Don, if you don't mind, I'd like to start first by showing Susan the basement."

A horrible thought crossed my mind. 'What if they're greeted by my friend, the rat?' After some quick thinking, I made an excuse for going first saying, "Here let me open the door. Sometimes it's hard to open when it's damp. I left a few things on the landing too, I wouldn't want you to trip over them."

Slowly opening it, I was relieved that my worry didn't come to fruition. I moved the broom and bucket I had stored on the landing, and flipped up the light switch. To my delight, my friend wasn't there.

"Here Delores, take this flashlight just in case you need it."

I watched as they went down the stairs and about half way, the light bulb at the bottom of the stairs began to intensify in brightness, the same as it did two weekends ago when I was examining the basement. It continued to get brighter then explode. Stopping where they were, Delores turned on her flashlight, and both turned to look up at the landing where I stood, waiting for me to give them a logical explanation.

"The same thing happened to me the first weekend I was here," I quickly remarked. "It must be a power surge. That's probably the answer with the age of the fuse box and wiring. I can see I'll have to keep a steady supply of light bulbs until I get it fixed. Here, let me change it."

I didn't want to add more mystery to their examination of the basement, but I didn't think they knew that much about electricity, and didn't realize a surge couldn't have caused that. It was a lie. After changing the bulb, I returned to the kitchen where Don was waiting.

Looking up at me he remarked, "I heard that excuse you gave them about the light bulb bursting. No way:"

"I know. But I didn't know what else to say."

In about 10 minutes they emerged from the basement.

"Well Sue, what do you think about Ray's project down there?" Don asked.

"You're right. It's pretty challenging, to say the least."

We followed them as they left the kitchen heading for the bathroom where I had my incident with the hot water.

"Is this where you experienced the water change?" Sue asked, as she stood next to the tub for a few minutes.

"Yes, right here. Are spirits confined to a room, or are they free roaming throughout a house, like the ghost I saw in the living room?"

Trying to sense something psychic, she replied, "That depends, sometimes they're confined to a room where they died. I've seen it both ways. Where were you when you saw the apparition of the woman? ...and Ray, we prefer the word apparition or manifestation over the term ghost. Ghost has the connotation of being dramatic, or something that's sort of a Hollywood explanation."

"Let me show you." Returning to the living room I pointed to where I was the night it occurred, "I was in my sleeping bag right here on the couch when the wind rattling the windows woke me out of my sleep," pointing with another gesture. "I saw a faint shadow coming from the dining room, and as it moved through the living room coming closer, it became more visible. I rubbed my eyes trying to wake myself, and saw the woman dressed in black, wearing a black bonnet. There was a white strip across the front, just like the woman in the carriage. In fact, that's who I thought she was. What really shook me up, as she passed the moon-lit window, I could actually see through her. She looked as though she was... " I paused, almost embarrassed to say it, "transparent: I could see right through her."

"Did she seem to be aware of your presence?" Sue asked.

"No, that's the strange part about it."

"What do you mean?"

"She didn't appear to be walking. She more or less glided across the floor. As she passed the couch, she never looked down at me. It was as though I wasn't there.

I watched as she went straight to the stairs and briefly pause, then turned as if she was examining the room. At that point it still didn't look like she was aware of my presence. Then she slowly went up the stairs."

"Could you see her face?"

"Yes, that's when I realized she wasn't the same woman from the carriage. They were dressed alike, but she looked to be very young, maybe 20.

The woman in the carriage was much older. I would say probably in her late 40s or early 50s, it was hard to tell."

"What did you do then?" Sue asked.

"I quickly got out of my sleeping bag and went to the bottom of the stairs. I yelled out to her- "Who are you? What do you want?" But she didn't answer. I know if she could have, I'm sure she would have realized by the frightened tone of my voice I was there. My voice cracked and must have sounded like a kid that whistles when he walks by a cemetery at night. Scared, but acting brave so anything that's potentially harmful would give whatever may be lurking, second thoughts about challeng- ing him. The weird part about it, by the time it took me to get to the bottom of the stairs, she should have already been past the landing or wherever she was going. I yelled again- "Who are you?"

Standing on the landing, she slowly turned her head and looked down at me as though she just recognized my presence." I paused for a moment from telling my experience, remembering how she looked at me then continued, "She had the saddest expression on her face__ a look that was almost pleading. A look as if she was beckoning me to follow__ a look that I'll never forget.

She paused, then turned to the right and went into the closet with a window. Funny thing, I never heard the door open or close, and it has a loud squeaky hinge."

Don asked, "What do you mean by a pleading expression on her face? You mean like a look of wanting you to help with something? Did you follow her up the steps?"

"Yes, but the fear and anxiety of confronting a ghost, sorry Sue, I mean the apparition, was the determining factor for not following her right away. In any other circumstance with an expression like that, I would have abandoned my own safety and never hesitated. After I got back in my sleeping bag, I tossed the event around in my mind. It never dawned on me that she might not be able to speak. Maybe that was the only way she could communicate without a medium."

Don directed his next question to Sue. "I thought spirits were sometimes heard moaning or crying, sometimes even laughing? How could they do that without a medium, or the ability to speak?"

"This isn't what you would call an exacted science Don. Sometimes, a spirit that wants you to help them can have a facial expression, as you said, sometimes pleading, sometimes sad, sometime fear- or even sometimes happy."

"Happy at dying:" Don asked.

"Yes, I had an occasion where a woman was terminally ill and bed-ridden for two years. She would manifest herself to her husband on occasion in a dressing mirror in their bedroom with a smile.

That's when he requested my services; just to make sure he wasn't going crazy or senile."

Sue then got back to my encounter. "Ray, what did you do then? Did you go upstairs?"

"Yes, I got up slowly not knowing whether I should tempt fate or just return to the comfort of my sleeping bag and leave it alone until morning.

After staring at the top of the stairs, I finally got up enough courage and decided to go up. As I slowly climbed the steps, the hairs on the back of my neck began to rise just like the description Frank gave me about his sister. The closer I got to the landing, the more they stood up. I wanted in the worst way to retreat but curiosity got the best of me and I went all the way to the top. As I slowly opened the door, the hinges made a creaking sound and I felt a light breeze across my face. The same way it had the first weekend I was here. To top it off, the full moon shining through the window from behind the tall wind-blown trees, cast eerily moving shadows on the wall of the closet.

I thought at first I was hallucinating when I saw several bolts of cloth leaning against the wall in one corner, and for a second I thought I saw what appeared to be a toddler's leg. He was in the sitting possession, with his leg sticking out from behind the bolts of cloth. It was as if he was hiding, playing a game, and I heard what I thought was a crying child. Those things weren't there that afternoon. Taking my eyes off the corner for a second, I rubbed them, and when I looked again, they were gone. The room was empty. Taking a last minute scan of the room, I closed the door then re-opened it just to make sure it was my imagination.

Going back down the stairs, I turned several times to reassure myself there was no one following me, spirit or human. I returned to my sleeping bag and after about an hour, I drifted off to sleep. In the morning, I felt a little braver when I climbed the stairs to examine the closet. After opening the door, it was the same as when I looked during the night- empty."

After discussing my chain of events at the bottom of the steps, Sue seemed impressed at my description and started slowly climbing the stairs with Delores following. Don and I watched as they went up, and saw Sue suddenly stop just short of the landing.

"What is it?" I asked aloud.

I thought briefly that somehow my friend the rat possibly got upstairs meeting them at the top. Suddenly, Sue turned almost knocking Delores down; trying desperately to get back down the stairs. Don and I looked at each other in surprise at what appeared to be a frightened reaction, wondering what was wrong. When she reached the bottom of the stairs, her face was pale and had a frightened look. Trembling, she glanced back up at the empty landing. She seemed severely shaken by the event and wasn't steady on her feet, and I know Delores must have been concerned wondering what was wrong.

Taking Sue by the arm, I led her to the living room where she sat down, and in a few minutes she looked a little steadier but was still pale.

I frantically asked, "Are you alright? What happened up there? You look a little pale. Let me get you a glass of water."

"Thanks Ray, I'm sure I'll be fine."

I returned from the kitchen, and she took several sips before getting back a little color. She remarked, "I'm sorry Delores for almost knocking you down, but I felt this terrible urgency to get back down the steps. It felt like someone had taken over my body without me being prepared."

"What do you mean, not being prepared?" Don asked.

Delores replied, "Well, when we have a séance, we make ourselves ready by allowing our body a few minutes of meditation. This prepares us before accepting the spirit. That didn't happen in this case, the spirit sort of leapt into my body, I was totally unprepared. It's something new to me. I've never experienced this before."

"What do you think it means?" I asked.

"I'm sure it's someone that wants me to help her with a decision between whatever the problem is upstairs, and what's going on downstairs, as if it's a life and death situation. The stairs seem to be a barrier she can't breach between the two things that are happening. Something's going on upstairs, and something's going on downstairs at the same time."

We never mentioned to Susan about the two men fighting in the living room that George told us about, and looked at each other, realizing Adda's spirit was torn between finding her child and Levi being killed by Daniel downstairs. They were two separate incidents that must have been happening simultaneously.

Chapter 12

It was getting late. George expected me at 4:30, and I didn't want to disappoint him. As I was getting into my car, Frank and June pulled up.

"June, everyone's inside. I'm going to pick up George. Come on Frank!"

As we were driving, Frank brought up the question of Sue's ability,

"Has she ever helped with any crimes?" he asked.

"I don't know Frank. I just met her for the first time today. Knowing what Delores can do, anyone that she says has the same ability is good enough for me. What's the big secret with what your wife experienced walking past the old barn?"

"Well, since she's already in the house and probably told them, I might just as well be tellin' you. When she was walking the dog on Tuesday evening, it began thundering and lightning. Turning back for home, she was passing the old barn when a carriage pulled up right in front of the old section. She said a man and woman got out."

I Interrupted. "Did she say what they looked like? I mean, what were they dressed like?"

"She said, at first she thought they were Amish, but she didn't recognize them from the Amish we know. She said the hair on the dog stood up, and her tail puffed out like a frightened cat. She didn't know what to do. She said the dog was goin' crazy, just absolutely crazy, pullin' on the leash; trying hard to get away from there. The dog finally broke loose and skedaddled for home," he gave me a look as if I would think he wasn't telling the truth then continued, "I was asleep on the recliner when the dog woke me up. She was just a howling and scratching at the door, just' tryin' to get in. When I opened it, she ran straight passed me headin for the bedroom, and hid in a closet. I went to see where she was, and when I opened the closet door, she was just a shiverin' and whimpering. I pulled back some of the clothes that were hanging in the closet, and she growled at me as if something was comin' after her. I wondered where June was, and as I was gettin' on my jacket to go find her, when she come a runnin' in the house. I asked what was wrong, and told her, she's pale as a sheet, like she just seen a ghost. She was shakin' like hell just like the dog and told me she thought she did.

When I asked what happened she told me, 'A carriage pulled up in front of the barn and a man and woman got out. The couple looked to be in their late 40s, or early 50s. They were both dressed in black, just the way you described them- like Quakers. When the man opened the barn door, the woman standing next to him looked up and screamed. As June said, 'A blood-curdling scream, then just stood there staring, looking up as if she was looking at the rafters.' She said that's when the dog finally broke free and headed for home. June began to run down the hill and looked back and saw the man standing there looking up too, as if he was examining the rafters. I told her to sit down and I would get her shot of brandy because she was still pale as a sheet. She said, 'Let me catch my breath first, I just ran all the way down the hill from the old barn.'

What he told me sent my curiosity reeling, and I wondered if we were going to expand on the answers this evening.

After picking up George, we went back to the house, joining the others. They were already in the kitchen and just as Frank figured, June had already related her story. Everyone was sitting around the table except Sue. I noticed she was examining the broken cabinet door from the previous weekend.

Acknowledging our entry, Delores remarked, "Ray, you'll never guess what happened to June this week?"

I replied, "Frank already told me."

Noticing the curiosity of Sue examining the broken door, I asked, "Sue, if a spirit can do that kind of damage to a wooden door, would it be farfetched that they could hurt or even kill a person that's living?"

"I guess that depends on the severity of their resolve. The spirit that did this obviously has that kind of power."

"Then, what Don said about me having Daniel standing behind me with a hatchet wouldn't necessarily be dramatic."

"No, I guess not. Delores telling me about the activity during the séance last week is one of the reasons I wanted to come. I also wanted to examine the mysterious blue bottle Delores told me about. Not to discourage you about the property, but if we can't end this haunting, the only other way to free the spirits would be to tear the house down."

"You're right, that's not very encouraging. Are we to assume the people at the barn are not hostile, but only Daniel that's in the house is?"

"So far, the people at the barn didn't try to harm you or June. You mentioned the Quaker that came to your door wasn't threatening. Isn't that correct?"

"Yes, he wasn't at all hostile. He only looked angrily at me as he went by the barn. When I spoke to him at the front door, he only seemed confused. I'll say again, your prognosis of tearing the house down isn't very encouraging."

"No, I guess not. Let's see if we can find out more. Shall we get started?"

Everyone seemed to have their own opinion of what happened to June this week, and I was anxious as the rest to get on with the séance. From what Susan had experienced on the stairs, we knew Levi was not killed outright, but was yelling for help. With everyone's mind working in the same direction, we seemed to be making headway.

The room was ready to go with the candles set around, and the blue bottle was in the middle of the table. We seated ourselves in the same positions we were the week before, and Sue being the sixth person with more psychic ability than George, took a seat on the opposite end of the table from Delores. I lit the candles and turned out the lights.

Delores and Sue began by closing their eyes and lowering their heads, going into a deep trance. We were all looking nervously at one another, waiting for something to happen focusing on Delores; thinking Adda would be the first to speak.

I looked at the opposite end of the table at Sue, and between the two of them, she seemed to be the first one entering the spirit world. Her long hair slightly fluffed up as if a spirit had gently entered her body, and within a few moments Delores's hair did the same. Something seemed different, definitely different- eerily different. Delores seemed to enter the spirit world much quicker than last week. Was it the fact that Susan's extra power was adding more energy to the group when we held hands? __I didn't know.

June already had the paper on the table with the questions we wanted to ask, and with her experience during the week she quickly took over the séance as if she'd been doing it for years.

"Adda are you present?" she asked. The blue bottle slowly turned to the paper on the table with the word *YES*.

"Will you speak to us tonight?"

Again, the bottle gently turned a complete revolution then stopped, pointing to the word *YES*. With everyone wide eyed, there was silence for a few seconds- a deafening silence. We looked at each other anticipating what was going to happen like the séance last weekend, but weren't sure in which direction it would come, or whether it would be violent and rather not see it happen.

Suddenly, in a different voice, Susan replied- "Yes, I'm here."

It seemed as though Adda was drawn to Susan, the stronger of the two psychics. We were surprised at the change and realized Delores for some reason was passed over.

Suddenly, turning our attention at Susan, June quickly asked, "Why were you home alone with your son?"

Adda in a lamenting voice replied, "Joshua's sick. He's so sick. I told Levi to go without me."

With our focus on Susan and Delores, we never realized George was possessed and spoke almost simultaneously. His voice sounded the same as it had the previous week- the voice that belonged to Levi.

"I don't feel comfortable leaving you here alone with Joshua being sick," Levi's voice replied, "I know how frightened you are during a thunderstorm with a lot of lightning. Maybe I should stay home?"

"I'll be fine. Try to get back as soon as you can, please!"

June quickly asked, "Levi, where were you going?"

"I'm going to our Wednesday meeting, we're going to talk about a house raising for Adam and his new wife. We have to plan on a day we'll start and what everyone's supposed to bring."

Don was sitting there observing like the rest of us, when all of a sudden a mist appeared over him, a strange mist- a mist that began to swirl in a circle. Faster and faster it spun until it formed a funnel that quickly swept down, entering his head. His hair dramatically stood up and his head drooped forward. Whatever it was had entered his body and in a brief moment, his head violently snapped back uncontrollably moving in a circling motion. The head movement suddenly stopped, and his eyes opened wide only exposing the whites.

In an instant, they suddenly turned red- a red that glowed like the hot end of a piece of steel a blacksmith would hammer into shape. His neck swelled to almost twice its thickness, then began pulsating.

With a complete transfiguration of his normal face, he seemed to be transfixed staring at the blue bottle. We were shocked at the activity, and made the séance last week pale by comparison. The distorted transition of Don's body was frightening, and an extremely tense moment passed. He obviously became one of the mediums for a spirit, but for which one? Could it be Daniel or just the hateful emotion that burned within Daniel? What the hell! We looked at each other surprised. So much had taken place so far, but this was really getting to be frightening. Just then, a deep groan came out of Don's mouth- a groan that seemed to emanate from deep inside of him- a groan that frightened the hell out of all of us who weren't possessed. As Frank put it earlier, 'A, frighten-the- hell- out- of- us weekend.'

Don spoke in a growling voice still transfixed staring at the bottle, "When I know they're at the meeting, that's when I'll get my revenge."

Shocked at Don being involved and the angry tone of voice, June quickly asked the second question. "What does the barn have to do with the fire in the house?"

Don turned to June and his eyes seemed to get a deeper red, as if he took offense to her question. With that look of anger, I feared the spirit we aroused was a spirit that was dangerous, and I was right. A drawer suddenly opened crashing to the floor spilling its contents.

Slowly, a two-pronged fork rose from the strewn implements, then hurled itself across the room imbedding in the plaster wall.

This was probably the spirit responsible for me getting burned by the sudden hot water change in the shower, and was most likely the one that was slamming the doors and drawers, opening and closing them violently the weekend before. That kind of power, to be able to split a wooden door, was giving me cause for alarm. I was worried that there could be some sort of harm to Don or someone else in the room, and wanted to break the séance. I was afraid of the consequences to Don if I broke the séance with the evil spirit still in his body and wondered, 'Would it remain? Would it turn a friend into the monster that's now being displayed?'

Delores, still sitting in a semi-trance began to speak as a toddler crying, "Momma, Momma, Momma."

Susan frantically cried out, "Joshua, where are you? Joshua, where are you?"

The table shook, and the blue bottle that was in the middle spun around several times in one direction, then suddenly stopped, and began spinning in the other direction. June seemed to be more per-sistent than frightened and had the courage Frank and I lacked. At this point, the look on Frank's face reaffirmed him not wanting to be invol-untarily volunteered, and I was beginning to feel the same. It looked as though he was ready to make a dash for the front door any second, and I knew if he did, I wouldn't be too far behind.

George spoke in Levi's voice, screaming, "I know you'll be burning in hell for your sins this day Daniel." Moaning, George grabbed his knee.

All this was happening so fast, like it was choreographed- like a stage play. I quickly asked, "Adda, who was in the carriage by the barn?"

She replied, "Daniel's parents. They were coming to warn me but they were too late." She paused for a moment, "The roads are too muddy to be able to come by carriage very fast." In a lamenting voice again she continued, "It's been raining for days- for days now. Won't it ever stop?"

June quickly asked, "What danger were they trying to warn you of?"

Don angrily looked in her direction as if he was about to retaliate if she answered. I noticed the spilled implements in a pile on the floor, was as though something was moving them, trying to find just the right weapon to use against an offensive question. Another sharp instrument rose from the pile and hurled itself against the wall sticking in a cabinet. Realizing the danger, I jumped up from my chair, breaking the chain and yelled, "Enough! Enough! Be gone with you!" Then quickly turned on the light and blew out the candles. To my surprise, it worked, and I temporarily felt a little proud of my bold accomplishment. Seeing everyone that had been in a trance having difficulty recovering, I put my success aside and helped as best I could.

June, Frank and I were still shaken by what happened, but we began helping everyone trying to recover.

"Don, are you alright?" I asked, "You scared the hell out of us."

He shook his head and rubbed his eyes. He seemed to be having the hardest time recovering, but in a few seconds replied, "I'll be fine, I'm drenched with sweat, what happened?"

"We think you became possessed by Daniel. It was pretty traumatic," I said, then asked, "George, are you alright?"

Rubbing his leg replied, "I'm fine. I think I hurt my knee again though."

"Frank, do you think we can critique this thing at your house? I think it'll be a better atmosphere."

"Sure, give June and I a few minutes then come on down."

"George, should I drive you home now?" I asked.

"Not yet. I'd like to hear what took place."

"Don, you sure you're ok?" I asked.

"I'm fine. Let's get out of here. Not to insult your house Ray, but this place gives me the creeps."

After picking up the contents that were spilled on the floor, we left for June's and gathered around her dining room table.

"All right, who's going to be the first one to tell us what they were feeling? Why don't we start with you Sue?"

"Who possessed me? I don't know," she asked.

"You were possessed by Adda we think." June replied.

Delores asked, "Well, if she was possessed by Adda, who possessed me?"

"It was a voice of a young boy. I'd say about two or maybe a little older. You were crying and calling 'Momma! Momma! Momma:' Don't you remember anything?" June asked.

"I can remember smoke getting in my eyes and rubbing them trying to see. Someone was calling, 'Joshua where are you?' I heard it again and again. Then I heard her say, 'Levi I can't find him.'

"Can you remember where you were when you heard the voice?" June asked.

"I think I was hiding from the smoke behind some bolts of cloth. I must have been in the sewing room. I remember I couldn't get down the steps. The smoke was in my eyes, so I tried to hide from it in the closet. That must have been the apparition of the toddler's leg from behind the bolts of cloth you saw Ray. If that's the case, the pleading expression on the woman's face looking down the stairs at you could be what she was trying to communicate. Joshua was hiding from the smoke, and she wanted you to save him."

"That sounds logical, but why couldn't she find him?" I asked.

I looked at George. He seemed to be in deep thought. "George, do you have anything to add?"

"Yes, I just remembered something. It might be important." he replied.

You could tell he was searching his memory.

"What was it?" I asked.

"I think I mentioned to you before, but I don't know whether Susan knows. When I was about 10, I recall there was a fire in this house.

There was a child that died in that fire. I think he was 2 or 3 years old. Do you think they could be connected?"

I asked, "Why would you think the child that died in the house of Adda and Levi, would be relevant to the child that died in 1910?"

I looked at Susan, and she remarked, "I don't know Ray. If you would have let the séance continue, we may have found out."

"Well, with Don's violent possession, I didn't feel safe with continuing. When that fork flew across the room and stuck in the cabinet, I thought things were getting out of hand. Maybe I'll just seriously entertain the thought of tearing the place down as Don suggested."

"Don, what did you feel?" Delores asked. "Did you feel like you were in any danger with the spirit taking over your body?"

"No, not in any danger, but I began to feel strange, as if I was having an anxiety attack. Something like the instant rush you have when you're frightened. Then I was angry with a person, an anger that I can't imagine anyone could harbor. I remember it coming and going as if there were two people possessing me, one of anger and one of sorrow. They seemed to flash back and forth. Maybe they were responding differently because of the questions being asked."

Sue asked, "What was the feeling of sorrow? Do you remember?"

"It seemed very loving and a helpless feeling of remorse about something that was happening. Then I felt the other- a feeling of pure hate and revenge. A revenge that could produce the kind of reaction we experienced last weekend."

After our round table discussion, we decided to call it a night.

Getting up from the table June remarked, "It seems like we have more questions than answers. We'll have to be prepared to ask more questions tomorrow evening. You're not giving up, are you Ray? We're going to try again tomorrow, aren't we?"

"If everyone's agreeable I don't mind__ How do you feel about it George?"

"I'll be glad to help. Just pick me up about the same time."

I knew Susan was more than impressed with her conversations with George. Wanting to know more about his psychic ability, she asked if she could accompany me in taking him home. We left the others discussing the events of the evening, and walked George to the car.

On the way to his house, Susan kept asking him questions about séances he knew about from his ancestors. I was hoping she wouldn't make a nuisance of herself asking so many questions, and I was glad she stopped as we pulled into his driveway.

As we walked him to his porch, Sue apologized, "Sorry for all the questions George, but you're so interesting to talk to. You seem so casual about your ability."

"Well, it's just something some people have. Like I told Ray here, I didn't think I could talk in the spirit world, at least not like my grand-mother. I tried it years ago and wasn't very successful, but these spirits don't seem to have a problem with me.

If you want me to tell you more, why not come over tomorrow earlier, and we can talk about it."

Looking at me she answered, "I'd love to, if Ray will bring me."

"I don't have a problem with that Sue. What time do you want us to stop by George?"

"How about coming over after lunch?"

"We'll see you then."

Susan gave him a slight embrace of endearment, and before going inside he smiled saying, "Now that's somethin' I ain't had in years!"

Sue turned to look at him asking, "What's that George?"

"A beautiful young girl, huggin' me on my back porch."

She smiled, and we walked back to the car.

"You know Ray- I think you fell into something real nice here. These people are really sincere when they speak. And George- George, he's such a sweet old gentleman. I hope this isn't too much of a strain on him."

"I hope you're right. I asked Frank that same question last week. He said if George thought so, he wouldn't volunteer."

"Well, as I said, the people here seem to be more accommodating."

When we pulled into the driveway at Frank's, Delores and Don, were already standing at the door waiting for us. We said our goodnights then headed for the motel.

As we passed the same tavern we went to the previous weekend, Sue commented, "Look at all the people outside that place. It seems like it might be fun. Why don't we stop for a drink?"

"What do you think Delores__ Don? Should we let her see what country people are like on the weekend?"

"Ray, don't tell me you're an old stay at home person?" Sue asked.

"No, not at all, but you might find this place a little different."

We pulled into the crowded parking lot, with what seemed to be the same motorcycle group out front. Passing by them, they nodded as we walked by, remembering seeing us before.

We entered the bar which seemed to be more crowded than the weekend before, and wound our way through the crowd to the back of the room. Finding an opportunity just as a table became vacated, we sat down.

I noticed Sue looking around at the patrons tapping on the table in tune with the country music being played, and I had to lean toward her and speak loudly to be heard over the conversations and music.

"What do you think of this place?" I asked.

"Looks like it's a fun place- Want to dance?"

"Sure: Don, order me a beer when the waitress comes around. Sue, what do you want?"

Still looking around and tapping the table to the music, she replied by gesturing holding up two fingers, "Don, make that two."

We wound our way back to the crowded dance floor between people who were just standing next to their tables, tapping their feet. They were enjoying the music just as well as the people on the dance floor, but didn't want to fight the crowd to get there.

I held Sue's hand and her feet became immediately choreographed in tune with the music. I wasn't as astute with dancing and knew immediately I couldn't match her ability. I more or less stood stationary, swinging my body in time to the music, enjoying watching her. Giving me a reassuring smile, she let me know my lack of ability wasn't a problem. When the tune ended, we went back to an empty table. It appeared Don and Delores had the same idea to dance after we left and were returning to the table at the same time.

"Sue, how does it feel to be like a sardine in a can, trying to wiggle out a dance?" I asked.

"Well, the thought of enjoying the music and tapping your feet is what it's really about."

Because of the challenge of communicating above the conversations and loud music the same problem of trying to communicate as the week before, we decided to finish our drink and leave. After we arrived at the motel, Delores and Don retired to their room for the night, while Susan and I took a table in the breakfast room. Over a cup of coffee, we discussed a little more of my situation at the house.

"If Don's possessed again by Daniel, should I do what I did tonight-break up the séance?" I asked.

"I would give it a little more time and see what else we can find out. There are several points I don't understand. First, why did Levi, who had gone to a meeting, all of a sudden return to the house? Second, why are the people in the carriage seemingly transfixed on the barn, when in fact, they came to warn Adda and Levi of the potential danger that night with Daniel. Why didn't they go to the house?"

I asked, "You know, George brought up an interesting point tonight when he said he remembered the toddler dying in the fire in 1910. How would that affect what we're seeing?"

"It could be that Adda was swept into the more recent tragedy still thinking she could save Joshua."

"You mean like a second chance to save him?"

"Yes, sometimes spirits are so strong they can move from one tragedy to the next if it's happening where they're already residing, for lack of a better word. Whatever it is, I'm sure we'll find some resolve tomorrow night. With that thought in mind, I think it's time to turn in. Goodnight Ray. See you in the morning, and by the way, Thanks for the dance!"

With a chuckle I replied, "Goodnight Sue."

Chapter 13

I was up bright and early lying in bed thinking about a potential relationship with Sue. She seemed accommodating, and I didn't think it would be a problem. I thought, 'Oh well, it's something I could work on later.'

As I was getting out of bed heading for the bathroom, there was a knock on the door adjoining Don and my room. I opened the door and before Don could speak, I remarked, "I know, I know. You're ready to eat. So am I. I'll be down directly. Is Sue up yet?"

Delores sleepily replied scratching her head as she walked passed Don, "I called her room awhile ago, and there's no answer. She may have been in the shower or already downstairs in the dining room." Putting her open hand against her mouth to stifle a yawn she said, "We'll see you down there."

As I closed the door I replied, "Ok, see you then."

Exiting my room, Susan was leaving hers. After bidding each other good morning we went down in the elevator together.

At breakfast, Delores and Sue were buzzing about what we discussed the night before.

"You know Delores, George's statement about the toddler dying appears to be like a bridge connecting the two incidences. I wonder if that could be the connection. I hope it's something we find out tonight."

Delores replied, "I guess we'll see."

After breakfast, we headed for the farm.

"What can we do to help spruce up this place while we're waiting?" Sue asked.

Don sarcastically remarked, "If you see Cinderella's fairy god-mother, try stealing her magic wand."

We laughed. Sue, like Delores, seemed to dive into helping clean up the kitchen. Don and I finished cleaning up the bathroom and carried out the rest of the carpets from the dining room. About an hour later, satisfied with our accomplishment I said, "Delores, when we dropped George off last night, Sue asked if she could come over to his house this afternoon so he can tell her about some of his experiences. Do you want to come along?"

Don replied, "If you don't mind Ray, could Delores and I drop you and Sue off at George's and use the car? Delores and I want to go into town."

"That's fine with me."

After they dropped us off, we walked up the path to the back porch. Sue had only seen the place when it was dark and looking at the back porch remarked, "It's just the way I would have expected it would be."

George, seeing us on the path, came out on the porch to greet us.

"Good morning George. How's the knee?" Sue asked.

"It's fine. When I saw the car driving away again, I thought you might have changed your mind about stopping."

"No, Delores and Don wanted to go into town. I think they want to buy a few things to take back to the city. Things here are a lot less expensive."

"Well, come inside where it's a little warmer- kind of chilly today."

"That sounds inviting," Sue exclaimed.

I could smell the wood smoke blowing down from the chimney and knew the warmth from the fire in the wood stove would be comforting. Entering the kitchen through the back door, we both saw dirty dishes in the sink and on the counter.

"I'm sorry for the way the kitchen looks. I just didn't have the ambition to clean up."

"That's alright. I live alone and know just how you feel." I replied.

Sue asked, as she went to the sink and began washing the dishes, "George, how long have you been living alone?"

"My wife died about 12 years ago. I've been alone ever since." Looking at Sue he said, "I'm embarrassed at you doing my dishes, you don't have to do them."

"Well, you don't have to be embarrassed. I'm going to learn a great deal when you tell me about all your experiences. Let's start with the first question. How old is that blue bottle?"

Pulling out a chair sitting at the kitchen table he replied, "I can't rightly say. It was my grandmother's grandmother. She lived about a hundred and fifty years ago. I suspect it's even older than that."

"Did she always use the bottle?" Sue asked.

"No: Not that I know of. My grandmother told me sometimes she used a sewing needle with a thread attached."

"What did she do with that?" Sue asked.

"That's what she used to tell a woman that was pregnant if she was going to have a girl or a boy. They say she was pretty accurate."

"I'm interested in the blue bottle. What else can you tell me about it?"

"It would do the damndest thing. My wife didn't like it at all. She made me keep it in an old chest that belonged to my grandmother."

I was intently listening as Sue continued questioning and knew Delores would have relished listening as well.

She asked, "What do you mean do the damndest things?"

Moving the salt and pepper shaker together on the table, he looked up replying, "Somehow it would move by itself."

"You mean turn, like it did during the séance?"

"No, it would do worse than that. It went from the shelf on the hutch over there," pointing in that direction, "To my grandmother's old bureau with the dressing mirror in the next room. At first I thought it was my wife moving it out of the living room because I knew she didn't like it, but when she told me she thought I moved it, she started to wonder whether me or her were getting forgetful.

We watched it carefully one day, and realized neither one of us touched it. Sure enough, it moved again__ all by itself. For some reason it wanted to be near my grandmother's dressing mirror. After that, my wife asked me to break the bottle or throw it in the river. She was really upset. That's when she asked me to put it in the trunk, which I did. It's been there until I took it out for the first séance."

Sue was finished the dishes attentively listening then asked, "I wonder whether the bottle has some sort of mystical power of its own and not just the spirits that were moving it?"

"That's interesting. I never thought of that. Sounds like it might have," George replied.

Before we realized it, the conversation with Sue's questions wore into the late afternoon. Like a strange thirst she couldn't quench, she kept asking more.

"I hope Don realizes the time and get's back soon," I said.

"I don't think that's a problem. Delores wouldn't miss the séance tonight for anything. Do you think you're still up to it George?" Sue asked.

"Yes, I feel pretty good- a little hungry right now, but I feel pretty good."

Sue, not realizing her imposition got up from the table. "I'm sorry George- let me fix you some lunch!"

"You don't really have to, but I wouldn't complain," he said with a smile. "The Campbell Soup's on the shelf right above the sink. I think there's some chicken noodle there too. The pot's right there in the oven."

I got up to assist asking, "George, where's the crackers?"

He replied, "I think I ran out. Soup's fine. Aren't you having any?"

"No, I think Don will be here soon."

Within the half hour, the car pulled into the driveway. I helped George put on his jacket, and we walked him to the car.

Sue remarked to Delores, "I hope your afternoon was enjoyable shopping."

"Yes, it was. I bought a few things to take home. That antique store is really something."

George added as we walked to the front door, "A few years ago, the people around here would have called it junk and threw it away."

"Well George, did Sue pester you all afternoon with questions?" Don asked.

"No: as a matter of fact, I'm ahead of the game. They made me lunch, washed and dried my dishes, and put em' away."

Sue said, "Delores, George told me an interesting story about the blue bottle. I think, from what he said, the bottle may have some mystical power of its own. It's not only able to move on the table during the séance but from room to room."

Don skeptically remarked, "What? Move from room to room as like levitate, move all by itself!"

"It appears like it," Sue replied. "According to George, it somehow always winds up on his grandmother's dressing table.

He told us his grandmother would sit at her dressing mirror combing out her long hair quietly chanting phrases with the blue bottle in front of her."

Delores said, "That's interesting. Does he remember any of the phrases?"

"I never asked," Sue replied. "Maybe after we finish with this problem, we can try to figure out what kind of power it really has."

Pulling up to the house, I parked in front of the barn and we started up the lawn just as Frank and June pulled up.

"Are we ready to start?" Frank asked.

"I guess so Frank. I hope we can finally find some answers."

We got to the porch and after unlocking the door, I looked to the edge of the woods. The sky was an orange color again, slowly fading into darkness behind the trees.

"I'll set up the candles Ray. Will you arrange the chairs?" Sue asked.

Everyone took the same seats as the night before, and Sue, along with Delores, lowered their heads, waiting for the right moment before beginning. In a soft tone June spoke, focusing her question at Susan.

"Adda, are you with us tonight?"

Her long blond hair fluffed up slightly as did Delores's, and we understood they were both ready to receive questions. June had a paper in front of her with what we agreed to ask the prior evening, but before she asked, Sue, in Adda's voice, began lamenting, "It's been raining for days, won't it ever end?" Repeating herself over and over.

Seemingly speaking aloud about her private thoughts she continued, "Joshua is so sick. Hurry back Levi. Please hurry back. All this lightning and thunder scares me."

George became possessed almost immediately after hearing the voice of Adda, and June seized on the moment.

"Levi, did you stay at the meeting until it ended?" she asked.

"No: after I got there, I spoke to Daniel's parents and asked where he was. They told me he was supposed to be there already, but didn't know why he wasn't. I had a strong feeling there was something his parents were worried about. About 15 minutes after I arrived, the meeting started. I looked around the room and realized Daniel still wasn't there. Then a sudden fear came over me. I didn't know why, but I had a feeling Adda was in danger and hurried out the door. My horse was still saddled in the meeting house barn, and I left at a gallop to get back home. It was still raining hard with bright lightning flashes, and the road was so muddy I had to slow down to almost a walk at times. I was afraid the horse might lose his footing and fall at the sharp turn just before crossing the bridge with all the mud."

"Did you suspect Daniel was at your house?" June asked.

The first reaction of the night; the blue bottle shook then spun, pointing to the word *YES*.

He continued, "I had a feeling that something bad was going to happen to Adda."

At that point all of us noticed a small mist over Don's head once again. It moved in a troubling circle this time then shot down entering his body. He began to shake as though he was having convulsions, and his head fell forward onto the table. I was about to reach over to shake him to see if he was alright, when his head slowly rose, staring at the bottle.

Startled, I snatched my hand back, and his head began moving in a circular motion the same as the night before. His eyes rolled back exposing the white, then suddenly became a deep red, filled with anger. His neck began to pulsate again and grew to almost twice its normal thickness. With his neck still pulsating, he slowly looked at each one of us. His frightful expression was as though he was intending to extract some sort of revenge- a punishment for stirring up the unpleasant act of his past, and was trying to decide which one of us to direct his rage toward first.

Groaning with a voice from deep inside, he began to speak, "When I know they're at the meeting, that's when I'll get my revenge. Levi holds her captive in this house and keeps her tied to this marriage with having Joshua. I know she loves me."

We were hearing Daniel's thoughts as to why he began to hate Levi and the house Levi built to give refuge to the woman Daniel loved.

"Did you do something to Levi?" I asked.

The bottle spun around several times before pointing to the word *YES*.

"What did you do that night?" I quickly asked.

Turning to look at me he said, "I saw Levi ride up to the barn, and knew he must have seen the house on fire. I grabbed a hatchet that was lying next to the fireplace and hid behind the front door." After saying it he stopped, surveying each of us, as if he was daring us to challenge his resolve.

I asked, "What happened next?"

Turning to me again, he looked as though it was gratifying for him to make his next statement.

"Levi ran in yelling, 'Adda are you in here? Get our son and get out of the house, it's on fire.' His voice took on a saddened tone, "I didn't know it. I was shocked Adda was still in the house. I thought she would be at the meeting with Levi. I never heard her until after I set the fire. I could hear her calling for Joshua, and tried to help but it was too late."

Don's head seemed to fall forward, and he began crying and moaning as though he was lamenting starting the fire killing the person he loved.

Speaking, making his thoughts audible, he said. "I'm sorry Adda. I didn't know you and Joshua were home." His tortured soul turned almost immediately with a gratifying anger saying, "But I'm not sorry for what I'm going to do to you, Levi."

George groaned then grabbed his knee saying, "You'll be burning in hell for what you've done this day Daniel," Then his head fell forward.

It was all happening so simultaneously, we were looking back and forth wondering who was going to speak next, trying not to miss the dramatic scene unfolding right in front of our eyes.

"What did you do to Levi? Did you murder him?" I asked.

"Yes!" he said in a self satisfying tone. "I was hiding behind the door when he came in. I swung the hatchet, but he moved and I only hit him on the knee. We fought, and he struggled to get the hatchet out of my hand, but already being wounded he couldn't. He's bigger and stronger, but he couldn't get to his feet. That's when I was able to hit him several more times. I stood over him with his eyes staring up at me, almost pleading for me to help Adda instead of sparing his life. I could still hear her screaming, 'Joshua where are you?' I looked down at him again and swung the hatchet striking him on the side of the head. He just lay there helpless and bleeding with his eyes wide open looking at me. I suddenly felt sorry for him, remembering all the times we had growing up together. With Adda still screaming, trying to find Joshua and calling Levi's name, I became panicked."

Susan spoke out loud again. "Joshua, where are you? I hear you crying, but I can't find you." She paused briefly then said, "Won't someone help this poor boy?"

She didn't say Joshua, what boy was she talking about? Could it be the kid who died in the fire in 1910? Had she somehow been swept into the more recent tragedy trying to help her own son? Just as we were beginning to understand what was happening, a faint smell of smoke was present. It wasn't from the candles. What was it? Suddenly it came to me- it was the same smell of burning wood from George's stove. It seemed as though the odor was getting progressively stronger.

"Frank, do you smell wood burning?" I asked.

"Yes I do. Do you smell it June?"

"Yes, and it's beginning to get warm too. Don't you feel the temperature difference?"

"Now that you mention it, it does feel warmer." Frank said.

"Adda, are the people in the carriage relatives? If they are, who are they?" June asked.

"They're Daniel's parents coming to warn me about Daniel. They've been suspicious about his violence the last few weeks, and felt he may try to do something to Levi and me. They came to warn us about his anger."

"What does the barn have to do with that night?" I quickly asked.

The room became warmer, and the smell of smoke began to be overwhelming. The table began to shake, actually coming off the floor. When it became steady again, the bottle began to shake, spinning in an erratic motion- first one way, then another. It seemed as though it was asked to answer an intolerable question. Finally, after spinning around several complete revolutions, it flew off the table on its own, smashing against the kitchen wall.

Startled, we jumped up and unlocked hands, but the spirits that entered our world wouldn't be silenced. I yelled, "Enough! Enough!" But unlike last night, the spirits had their own agenda- an agenda to unlock the truth- the truth they never knew about each other following their untimely deaths.

Adamant to get an answer, I persisted in a louder authoritative tone. "Did the barn have something to do with the fire in the house that night?"

The mist, that entered Don's head exited, then moved rapidly around the room. Once again the cabinet doors and drawers began opening and closing in a furious manner as they did the night before. Unlike last night when they began to open and close slowly, then progressively increase, it was rapid activity immediately. June, Frank and I watched in horror as a drawer with kitchen implements fell to the floor once again. In a few moments the instruments on the floor were moving as though someone was searching through them, much like anyone looking for the right instrument when preparing a meal. In horror we watched as a butcher knife rose from the pile and flew through the air just missing my head by fractions- this time causing me to duck. It was thrown with such force it stuck in the wall behind me by several inches.

Frank yelled out, "That's enough! June, let's get the hell out of here before one of us gets hurt."

I was inclined to believe he was right, it was getting dangerous. I obviously angered Daniel, who was trying to kill me for asking the question. The mist circling the room again returned over Don's head, but this time didn't enter his body.

"I'm not going to shame my family. I'll end it myself," Daniel said.

The mist moved rapidly to the kitchen window briefly pausing; then disappeared. With the mist gone, Don came out of his trance, and his head fell forward onto the table. With Daniel's spirit leaving, everyone was slowly coming out of their trance, trying to recoup from the possession.

"Are you alright Don? Is everyone else ok?" I asked.

George was having a difficult time getting back to normal, and I went to the sink to get him a drink of water. Standing at the sink, I looked out the window. Startled, I jumped back. A man sheltering his eyes was peering back through the window at me. Surprised, I snapped my head back thinking it might be Daniel who somehow manifested himself into human form. After a closer look, I realized it wasn't Daniel. It was the same Quaker who came to my front door asking for directions the first night I arrived. Yes, I was certain he was the same person- the person driving the carriage. The father of Daniel that Adda told us was coming to warn her of Daniel's rage.

"June quick, come to the window and see if this man is the one you saw at the barn?"

She hurried to the window with Susan and Frank peering out. "Yes, that's the same man, and the woman in the carriage looks like the same woman."

Concentrating on the man, I hadn't noticed the carriage parked on the front lawn. It was indeed the same woman and carriage that was parked in the same spot when he came to the door the night I arrived. The man was holding his hat in his hand, shaking his head looking off the front porch. He seemed confused, as though he was still trying to figure out where he was. When he turned around, he looked in the window again shadowing his eyes with his hands trying to see if anyone was inside. We were all at the window, and it was obvious he couldn't see us. Suddenly we heard a knock at the front door, and looked at each other wondering who was going to be brave enough to answer it.

I stepped forward with everyone behind me, but when I opened the door, there was no one there. The Quaker and the carriage were gone. They had completely disappeared.

Hurrying across the lawn to the barn, Susan said, "I think that may be the connection with the haunting. That may be where the mist went. Ray, were you parked in front of the older section the night you first saw the carriage?"

"Yes. Why?"

"Move your car to the same position as it was that night."

I moved it without hesitation asking, "Why are we doing that now?"

Sue replied, "Open the barn door. Maybe we'll have that answer."

I opened the door as she asked, and all of us stepped inside. Although there were no new bales of hay and hadn't been for many years, the odor of freshly cut hay filled the night air. There was no storm, but looking out from inside the barn, we could see lightning flashes and the sound of a heavy downpour hitting the roof- eerie to say the least.

A chill went up my spine and I knew I couldn't be alone with my feelings. We were looking at each other wondering what we were going to experience next, realizing we were re-living the night of the tragedy. The thunder and lightning were as real as the storm the first night I arrived. With periodic flashes of lightning every few seconds, we scanned the room imagining suspicious shadows lurking in almost every corner. Don let out with another groan as he did when Daniel's spirit entered his body in the kitchen. We thought the spirit had left him, but it became obvious it either didn't- or he was being repossessed after entering the barn.

With continuous flashes of lightning, we looked up and saw a figure of a man standing on a barn beam above us with a rope around his neck. I turned to look at Don, just to make sure it wasn't him, and to my relief; it wasn't. We expected him to speak, but there was only silence as he stood with his outstretched arms in front of him, as if he was contemplating some sort of action. With the next flash of lightning, shockingly, we saw the form of the man above us step off the beam.

In the darkness that followed the lightning flash, we could hear a snap, like a small tree branch, and the swinging weight of a body against the squeaking of a tightening rope. With the next flash of lightning, we looked up and saw what must have been the real body of Daniel hanging. To our surprise, his eyes opened and he looked down scanning us. His eyes blazing red with anger, a deep brilliant red, a red that could only describe the flames in hell he was about to feel. He seemed to be angry at us for trespassing on his private self-execution but was powerless to do us any harm.

Don fell to his knees when the apparition hung himself, and we were worried that some harm had come to him. After helping him to his feet, we brushed the loose hay from his clothes and stepped outside. We saw a carriage light coming toward us, and as it passed, we could see the same man who was on the front porch. Again, as he had the first night I arrived, he was staring angrily at us and within a few hundred feet the carriage disappeared.

Sue excitedly commented, "Ray, quick! Move your car to the front of the newer section."

I did as she asked without question, and the carriage reappeared on the road once again, coming from the same direction. With the car moved, the carriage was able to pull up in front of the barn door, probably the way it did the night the tragedy took place, and the way it did when June was walking the dog. We watched with great intent as the couple we now know as Daniel's parents get out of the carriage and open the barn door.

After stepping inside, the woman looked up and let out a blood-curdling scream. She stood like a statue, frozen, staring up at her son as he hung there.

To avoid the family being disgraced, Daniel took his own life. His, as well as his parent's shadows began to fade. This must have been the frightening episode June saw during the week. There was no more to be said. Daniel's parents were too late.

We were able to see a mirage where Adda and Levi's house must have stood. It was almost completely consumed by the fire and was in the last stages of smoldering embers, slowly being extinguished by the heavy rain.

We finally had a complete picture of the reason for the haunting, and I was happy to have some answers. Was it solved completely? I didn't know for sure. Susan excitedly remarked,

"Wait! Someone's missing. Where's George? I could have sworn he was right here with us."

I hurried back inside the barn to look just to make sure he hadn't fallen through a soft spot in the floor. With all the frightening activity, it wouldn't have been impossible for us to miss him.

"He's not in here," I said in a panic, "Maybe he stayed in the house when we hurried out the door?"

Running back to the house fearing for his safety, we entered the kitchen. Somehow, the light was turned off again and the candles were relit, just as it had been for the séance. George was still seated at the table with his arms folded and his head resting on them as if he were asleep.

"I hope he's not dead!" I nervously shouted.

We shockingly looked around, wondering how or who reset the room for another séance. Looking at each other, I went to wake him when Delores grabbed my arm.

"Look, look!" she exclaimed in an excited voice, "The blue bottle! The blue bottle! It's on the table. It's whole again."

Shocked, we stood there staring at the bottle. There it was- not smashed into pieces on the floor the way it was when we left for the barn, but intact, lying on its side, pointing at George.

"George, are you alright?" I asked.

No response. I tried to shake him thinking he was in a deep sleep, but a horrible thought went through my mind. Did we put too much strain on the old man? Was he dead? I felt for a heartbeat and it seemed strong.

"Maybe he's still in a trance?" Frank suggested. "Why don't we sit back down and try again Sue?"

"Good thought," she replied.

Surprised at Frank's level of wanting to get involved, I brought a pillow from the couch. Delores and June unfolded his arms and gently placed the pillow under his head.

"There, now let's take the same seats we had," Susan suggested.

After a few minutes she began. "Levi... Are you still here?"

George's head slowly rose from the pillow, opened his eyes, and seemed to become transfixed on the bottle.

"Yes, I'm here, Daniel has gone away."

Being focused on George we hadn't noticed, Susan became possessed once again by Adda, "I'm glad he's gone, but I feel sorry for his parents," she said.

"Why are you sorry for his parents?" Delores asked.

"They went home and committed suicide. They shouldn't have felt responsible for Daniel's evil deed," Adda through Susan replied.

"You don't seem panicked now. Are you at rest?" June asked.

"I'm hoping someone saves this poor boy. I think it's too late. I couldn't save him. He was hiding from the smoke behind the bolts of cloth in the sewing room. I couldn't find him. Yes, he's dead."

George spoke in Levi's voice, "Adda, It's not your fault. It's not your fault. It's not your fault."

As the voice slowly faded away, George came out of his trance shaking his head as if he were just awakening from a deep sleep.

"Are you ok George?" I asked.

"Yes, my knee doesn't hurt anymore. What happened?"

Susan went to his side, putting her hand on his shoulder she said, "You've been in the trance about an hour longer than we were. Do you remember anything?"

"I remember fighting with Daniel. Then, he seemed to disappear. I still heard Adda crying and pleading for someone to help her, but that too faded away. Was the blue bottle helpful?"

"It was more than helpful, but there's something we don't understand." Susan said.

"What's that?" he replied.

"During the séance a question was asked- what the barn had to do with the house. Reacting violently the bottle spun around several times, then flew off the table and smashed against the wall. We were so anxious to follow a mist that we thought might be Daniels spirit we never noticed you weren't with us. When we hurried back to the kitchen, we found you still here. Somehow, the shattered pieces of the bottle came together, and it was back on the table pointing at you."

Don picked up the bottle carefully examining it. "That's strange. I don't see a crack in it anywhere."

"Well, I told you it has the power to move on its own," George replied.

Looking at George with the statement he made, Don said. "I was a little skeptical when you said it George, but believe me, I'll never deny what I've witnessed."

Don asked, "Delores, what's your opinion on the bottle coming back together?"

"I didn't want to say anything, but with George telling us about it moving from room to room, I know now that it moved on its own in our motel room last night."

"It moved by itself?" I exclaimed.

"Yes: When we got back to the room last night, I put it on the dresser. When I woke up this morning, it was on the floor next to the front door. I thought Don had put it there not wanting to forget it, but he said he never touched it. George gave it to me, but I think it wants to stay with him. I'd be afraid to keep it now. It obviously has a great deal of power, and the power seems to be with George and his family."

"Why do you say that? Do you think the haunting is finished?" I asked.

"I think it may be. What do you think Sue?" Delores asked.

"Let's go over what we've learned. First of all, Daniels parents must have left the meeting after they saw Daniel wasn't there, and Levi leaving.

They no doubt went to the meeting in a carriage, and that's evident by the carriage going up and down the road, looking for the house Adda and Levi lived in. The reason for their delay in getting there was probably from the road being so muddy. The carriage wouldn't be able to travel very fast. As Adda remarked, 'It's been raining for days, won't it ever stop?' By the time they reached Levi's, the house no longer existed and had since been replaced by the current home. The barn that had been the original structure was added to and didn't appear the same because of the addition."

"Then how did they get from their time period to the present?" I asked.

"It could be that the spirit of Daniel remained fixed on this location. Remember, where he hung himself still exists and he used that place, still wanting to be with Adda. When she was transported into the future by the tragedy of the more recent fire, he wasn't able to bridge that gap."

"Then why is Levi in the same time period?" Frank asked.

"He isn't. Do you remember him saying I can hear you, but the house is different?"

"Yes, I remember."

"The only connection Levi has to the house as far as I can understand is him being murdered by Daniel and his love for Adda. His failure to heed Adda's warning, leaving her on such a stormy night might have something to do with it, but as I said, it isn't an exacted science. What's your opinion, Delores?"

"It could also be the anxiety of Levi trying to get here and not being able to save Adda and their son," Delores replied, "Like you said, 'It isn't an exacted science.' As far as the happenings at the barn, I think you're correct. That part is over with. As far as I can tell, the spirits in the house are no longer angry. Daniel's not here and will probably never return. Levi realizes Adda's in a different time period and since they can't seem to connect. Levi telling her, 'It's not her fault.' justifies in their mind the loss of Joshua, from her not being able to find him. With Levi's voice fading, I think Adda chose to go back to the beginning of their marriage, when she was the same contented spirit I felt when I touched the stone with the word 'Smythe' inscribed on it in the basement."

I looked at Delores warily saying, "Then that means Adda may always be present,"

"Not necessarily. Sometimes without the connecting spirits, they leave, or become dormant. That's something you'll have to wait to find out. If she isn't gone, at least she won't be demanding."

Don suddenly threw in a dig. "At least not like your ex." We laughed.

We were all still visibly shaken when Susan added, "It's amazing. We've just witnessed something that happened over 200 years ago. A tragedy of love and murder, and we were able to live it firsthand. Ray, I think your problems are solved. I have a feeling they're gone."

"Sue, without the power of you and Delores, I know we would have never solved this, I'm glad you came." Turning to Frank I asked, "Frank, do you have any doubts now about what your sister was going through?"

"No: but I realize what she meant by the hairs standing up on the back of her neck. Mine are still standing!"

"Mine too!" replied June.

"Come on George, I'll get you home now."

"Not so fast," he replied. "Last evening, I was invited for a cup of coffee with a shot of whiskey by Frank and his wife. I don't want to get cheated out of my fee. I knew my grandmother spoke in the spirit world, but she probably never had any experiences like this- like to scare me to death. I'm ready for that coffee."

We laughed as we got up from the table.

"I'm not quite finished with the spirit world yet either," Don revealed.

"What are you talking about? Do you still feel something?" I asked.

"No. The spirit world I'm referring to is in Delores's bag. I packed my own bottle of spirits for this trip."

"I think the coffee's a good idea. Frank, if you don't mind being the host," I said.

"June won't mind. I think scaring up these ghosts created a monster. She'll be looking for somethin' else that will scare the hell out of me," then laughed.

As we walked off the front porch to go to Frank's, I locked the door behind us saying, "It's October, and Halloween is two days away. Hopefully I'll be rid of my tenants who aren't paying rent as you said, Sue. I wonder if it's all worth it. Maybe I should have just done what Don suggested- tear the house down and start over again."

"I don't think so Ray," she replied. "If you need a little help, you can always call on me."

"You're welcome to come, but I've always been told that two women in the same kitchen are bad luck."

Everyone laughed.

Suddenly I had a serious thought, "Maybe it isn't such a laughing matter. Adda was still here, and that means something must be still holding her. What could it be? Could it be the toddler? Without mentioning it to the others, I realized if she manifested herself in any way, I'd have to have another séance to rid her from my home. The power of the blue bottle and Susan's ability may just do the trick. For now- I could postpone thinking about it. November was the month that Frank's sister was relieved of the problem- that was, until the next October, when the cool crisp air returns and the leaves begin to fall.

Hopefully, as Sue expressed, maybe my spirits are gone and I won't have to deal with them again- Or will I?

The End?????

Look for the sequel, *"Mist in the Blue Bottle,"* coming in the fall of 2020.

Other publications forthcoming by this author:

Coming in the fall of 2019: *"New Hope,"* a fiction murder mystery that takes place in a theatre in New Hope, Penna.

You can also look into a current publication by this author, titled *"Veronica." a* fiction murder mystery that takes place on Long Beach Island, New Jersey.